ANGEL IN DISGUISE

Ann Wiley

A KISMET® Romance

METEOR PUBLISHING CORPORATION
Bensalem, Pennsylvania

For Barb: Dreams, spun over crab legs and coffee, can come true.

And thanks to Aunt Mil for my first inspiration, "Bird Notes."

ANN WILEY

Ann Wiley, mother of four and grandmother of one, lives with her family in Albuquerque, New Mexico. Her favorite part of writing is creating well-matched characters.

PROLOGUE

The automatic doors of the University Hospital hissed open as the paramedics rushed the gurney through the doors and down the hall toward the emergency room.

"Trauma room three," someone shouted over the intense activity that circled the stretcher. Each member of the team zeroed in on his area of duty and expertise.

One of the paramedics spoke as they moved down the hall as a unit. "Witnesses say he was hit by a good-sized log that was tumbling through the rushing water. Said he could have gotten out of its way if he hadn't held on to the kid he was pulling out of the arroyo."

"And the kid?" one member of the trauma team asked as they quickly pushed the gurney down the hall.

"Lucky. Only a little waterlogged," the paramedic said.

Sodden, dirty clothes clung to the trembling. chilled body. His dark hair, slicked down with water, revealed strong, chiseled features in relief. On the left side of his face, from temple to jawline, a livid bruise, colored a deep purple, contrasted against the pallor of the rest of his skin. Efficiently but gently, the team slid the patient from the stretcher to the table. A low groan escaped the man's clenched jaw. He paled further, which seemed inconceivable to Sunny, as she took the IV bag from the paramedic and hung it on the stand.

As the paramedics cleared their equipment from the room, one of them called out, "Good luck, Lieutenant."

Lieutenant? Sunny wondered. But before she could follow the thought or ask who he was, she became involved with his care.

The lieutenant's dark gray eyes scanned the lifesaving equipment that filled the room before glancing at the face of each member of the trauma team who hovered over him. From the neck down they looked the same, except for height—all were clad in identical green scrub suits, a stethoscope dangling around each neck. Or at least they all looked identical until his eyes quickly returned to focus on the halo of golden-red hair. There was a name for that color. Refusing to allow the searing pain to overtake his mind, he deliberately concentrated on the woman standing next to him. Strawberry blond. That was the color of her hair. The lieutenant focused his unflagging attention on the woman as she moved to the end of the table.

Sunny removed the shoe and sock from his limp leg. His foot felt cold to her touch. The area below his left knee was the only part of his body not trembling. Choosing the pressed crease, worn almost white, as the path of least resistance for her scissors, Sunny began to cut away the dirty, dripping denim of his jeans.

She ignored the jostling of the other team members as they drew the patient's blood, monitored his blood pressure, and checked his respirations and heart rate, but she immediately glanced up as a tortured groan filled the room. The lieutenant's gaze locked on her face. Suddenly the detachment she needed to perform the taxing duties of a trauma-team nurse no longer existed for Sunny. His eyes, desperate and etched with pain, reached out to her, begging for understanding, for reassurance.

As she reached the bloodstained area of the material, her scissors barely slid under the denim due to the swelling flesh that filled the area. She eased the scissors under the fabric and cut up to the waistband. Out of the corner of her eye, she watched his clenched fist tighten further. Sunny tried to stifle her gasp as she uncovered the injury, but she knew he'd heard her. There was little reassurance anyone could offer him at this point.

Struggling up on his elbows, kinking the IV in his arm, the patient stared at his leg. Quickly Sunny helped him lie back down. Perspiration beaded his face and chest. She couldn't believe he was not screaming from the pain; his rigid control was almost frightening. Sunny wiped the sweat that trickled into his hair, and she blotted the livid bruise that swelled and distorted his features.

Drew closed his eyes against the glare. He had to block the image of his leg, but he knew he would never forget the sight—it would be etched on his brain in living color for as long as he lived. He needed to think of anything but that. No, not anything. The nurse. He opened his eyes and found his distraction.

Her hair smelled like spring flowers. *His knee was gone—it was a swollen mass of flesh.* Her doe-soft brown eyes were gentle with compassion. *He was losing control.* Her skin was perfect, free of makeup. *He'd never walk again.* A light dusting of freckles danced across her nose. *Everything was going black around the edges even though harsh, bright lamps glared down at him.*

As she wiped the sweat from his face, he grasped her hand. It was soft and feminine but offered surprising strength. The metallic taste of fear filled his mouth. Was his career as an undercover narcotics agent over?

Never before had Sunny been so distracted by a patient. It was as if she hadn't experienced years of training and trauma-team work. She felt like a fledgling.

Knowing that mere seconds could make a difference in life or death, she also realized that a patient's quality of life could be decided just as quickly. Yet something about this man reached deep inside her, erasing her normal detachment.

Gripping her emotions with steely force, Sunny glanced back at the man again. He regarded her with an unblinking gaze, searching, seeking—a ray of hope? Something she could not falsely give. With a certainty she didn't understand, Sunny knew he wouldn't want to hear a lie. Her thoughts raced in different directions. He was alive. He was stable, but would he ever have full use of his leg again? Could they even save the leg? She slipped her hand over his. Under her warm fingers, his fingers felt icy as they gripped hers.

Sunny jumped at the sound of the booming voice, "X ray. Get me an orthopedic surgeon. Wait! Find out who's on call, then we'll go from there. He's going to need the best orthopod there is—Johnson. See if you can get Johnson."

Sunny tuned out the rest of the doctor's demand. She knew from his request for the best orthopedic surgeon in the city that this patient—this man with the striking gray eyes—would need a sweeping stroke of good luck, also. The prognosis would not be good. She helped the other nurse cover him with warmed blankets, leaving only his lower left leg uncovered. But the warmth had no effect on his trembling body.

The doctor leaned over the patient. "Are you certain there isn't a family member we can call?"

At the negative nod of the patient's head, the doctor continued, "As soon as we view the skull X rays, I'll be able to give you pain medication, but first I have to make certain you don't have a concussion."

"No." The soft but vehement word was ground out between his clenched jaws.

"That's crazy! There's no reason for you to suffer needlessly."

"Not till I talk to the surgeon." His voice was a hoarse whisper.

Sunny observed the unspoken contest of wills between the inflexible director of the trauma team and the man who was obviously helpless, yet the patient displayed amazing courage and gritty determination. The moment the doctor nodded his assent, the patient's eyes returned to focus solely on her.

The orthopedic surgeon breezed in shortly, studied the X rays, and spoke to the patient. His soft, brief explanation seemed to satisfy the man. The medication the doctor ordered took the edge off the pain; his fists loosened and his jaw relaxed. The heavy sedation, which would have rendered most patients senseless, didn't affect his alertness as he continued to follow Sunny's every move.

As they wheeled him into surgery, Sunny felt his heated gaze cut through her like a laser. The beam hit an undefinable place buried deep within. She understood compassion—it was an integral part of her daily nursing—but this was different. She had looked past the patient and seen the man.

At the end of her shift, a force far greater than her good sense dragged Sunny up to the fourth floor. As she stepped out of the elevator onto the orthopedics unit, she saw a friend, another nurse, going off shift. "Can I talk to you a minute?"

"Sure, Sunny. What's up?"

"The lieutenant. Is he out of surgery?"

"Back from recovery about an hour ago."

"And?"

Her friend looked at her, but after a moment she said, "I wish he had some family here for him, but the chart says they're out of town."

Sunny nodded. "How is he?"

"The prognosis is not the best. The only good news is he kept his leg."

Sunny walked down the hall, paused, then pushed the door open. It swooshed shut behind her. Her heart wrenched at the sight before her. The bruise looked even darker now against his pale skin, and a frown covered his face even as he slept. An IV bag dripped fluid into his arm. He appeared so big, yet so vulnerable.

She reached for his wrist and felt his pulse before looking at the name on the identification bracelet. Andrew Williams. Turning his hand over, she held it lightly—her thumb tracing the vein on the back of his hand. He stirred and moaned, but after a moment he quietened. Sunny pulled up a chair and sat down to wait.

Pain dragged Drew from the dark safety of a drug-induced world he'd never before known. He forced his eyes to open. The room was dark except for a halo of light outlining her strawberry blond hair. Not certain she wasn't a figment of his imagination, he closed his eyes, then opened them again. The nurse from ER turned from the window and walked toward him. She reached out and took his hand in hers.

He could barely form the words in his meds-sluggish brain and get them past a mouth that felt like dry, woolly cotton. "Why are you here?"

Wanting to see him better, Sunny switched on a small light above the bed. She'd quickly learned in the ER that eyes responded even if the rest of the face remained unreadable. "Because I want to be here. Because I need to be here for you. Because I thought you . . . that you might need . . . ." She wanted to say, *me*; instead she said, "someone."

He nodded and squeezed her hand.

"I didn't want you to be alone."

Words formed in his mind, but he couldn't find the

strength to construct the sentences. His heart discarded them as impulsive, although he'd never considered himself reckless.

He nodded in understanding, acceptance. He was pleased she'd come. He didn't know what the future held, but for right now there was a bit of sunshine in his dark world.

Throughout the night she was there when he awakened. She appeared as a golden angel, meeting his needs before he knew what they were—a sip of water, an extra pillow to ease an aching muscle, the medication that would give him the freedom to escape the pain, if only for a little while.

The next time he awakened, it was light and she was gone. He groaned. His body felt as if it had been run over by a dozen boxcars. With that thought, breakfast and Dr. Johnson arrived.

"Lieutenant," the doctor said as he read the chart.

"Doc. Give me the facts. No sugar coating."

"Cold, hard facts?" Dr. Johnson walked to the window before turning back and speaking in a gentle voice. "I saved your leg, but that's all I could manage. I'm a doctor, not a magician. You'll never have full use of it. That joint will always be unstable, but you do have your own leg and not some prosthesis. I saved it so you could walk, and that's all you'll be able to do." Dr. Johnson took a deep breath. "And I'm sorry as hell I can't say I fixed it like new.

"Your superior called me this morning. I wish I could say you'll be back at work in a few weeks or even a few months. I can't. It'll have to be a desk job. I understand this is difficult to handle, and it'll take some time. But any more damage to the joint and you'll be on crutches or in a wheelchair for life." When the lieutenant didn't answer or allow a flicker of emotion to cross his face, the doctor said, "Let me know if you need anything. We'll talk again."

*   *   *

The next time Drew awakened, he looked toward the window where he'd seen her each time during the long night. He closed his eyes, his anticipation faded. He'd left word at the desk—she was not to visit again. A dark, foreboding cloud covered his heart. He didn't want anyone's pity. He'd made a choice. He'd had no choice. The doctor had told him what he feared. He'd never be as agile as he once was. His strength of mind remained. His strength of body was changed. Life as he knew it had changed.

In the space of twenty-four hours, Sunny's focus had altered. She'd waited all day to see Drew. Even though she was exhausted, there was a spring in her step as she neared his room. She'd napped a little last night in his room, then showered, donned fresh scrubs, and worked another shift. Sunny took her hand off the door as the nurse's words registered in her heart. Looking at her friend, she asked, "Are you sure that's what he said? That he didn't want to see me?"

Her friend nodded, and Sunny felt her shoulders sag. "Why?"

"He didn't say." The nurse walked toward the nurses' station. "He's not the type in my estimation to give anyone a reason for anything he does. I do know Dr. Johnson came in early this morning. The lieutenant refused his pain medication after that and only drank the coffee off his breakfast tray. When I was in his room a few minutes ago, he gave me instructions—to quote him, 'Tell that nurse from ER not to come in here again.' "

As though she had a slow leak in her anatomy, Sunny leaned against the wall, seeking support. She longed to go in his room, to defy his request, to gather him in her arms. Pushing away from the wall, she walked to the elevator.

ONE

Three years later.

Drew caught the flash of a black car speeding toward him. Gripping the steering wheel with both hands, he swerved to the left, jamming the accelerator to the floor and blaring the horn. There was nothing else he could do to avoid the collision. He braced himself for the inevitable.

Tires squealed and smoked. Drew's knee slammed against the steering column. The screech of tearing metal rent the air. The odor of burnt rubber and heavy exhaust floated up through his open window.

Stunned and angry, Drew sat quietly for a moment, recovering. Perspiration beaded his face.

Hearing the distant sirens, he loosened his cramped fingers from the steering wheel. Wiping his clammy hands down the legs of his jeans, Drew probed his throbbing knee, and swore.

The low groan of the siren evolved into a far-reaching wail as Mike turned the rescue unit in to a sharp U-turn. The call had come en route to lunch, momentarily postponing the ongoing argument between his partner and himself.

Mike glanced out the windshield and cleared his throat before barking into the small transmitter, "Our estimated time of arrival? With this traffic—four, make that five minutes." With the report of a two-car accident at the busiest intersection in Albuquerque, Mike knew lunch would be a long time coming.

Mind alert, his eyes scanning the traffic with precision, Mike shifted gears and changed lanes, slowly heading north on San Mateo Boulevard. Accustomed to the routine, he returned to the argument with fervor.

"I don't understand why you always refuse to come up to the ranch with me, Sunny. There are plenty of extra bedrooms."

Sunny pushed her aviator sunglasses farther up the bridge of her upturned nose. Her eyes scanned the traffic ahead of them. "For the last time, I'm not going. I am not about to intrude on your family, though I'd like to meet them sometime."

"We have four days off. You'd love it. You can escape this heat, jog in the cool mountain air, and enjoy Consuela's cooking. Besides that, I want you to meet Drew . . . and his boys, of course. They've heard a lot about you. You can even bring Prince Charming if you want." Without taking his eyes from the traffic, Mike asked, "Are you ignoring me?"

Sunny disregarded the smile in his voice and took a deep breath. "I'm doing my job, Mike. Remember, we *are* on duty. This traffic is horrific. It's going to take both of us watching for potential traffic problems to get us there within our ETA."

Knuckles clenched white on the steering wheel, Mike swore softly, braking as a car pulled in front of him.

"I hope this accident isn't too messy," Sunny said. "I'm starved. A big order of onion rings from Mac's sounds perfect."

"How you eat like that and keep your figure is beyond me."

"You've got that right, Mike. It is beyond you," Sunny agreed, automatically falling into a teasing routine with her partner that dated back to her days as an emergency room nurse.

Sunny had seen Mike occasionally during her years as a trauma-team nurse when he'd brought patients into the hospital. He'd asked her out, as he did every other nurse who had some semblance of beauty. Most were flattered by his attention. She, however, had merely been amused. Since they'd become EMT partners a few months ago, their relationship had been cemented into a close friendship. Sunny considered Mike the brother she'd never had, but then, she regarded all men that way.

There had only been one man who had eased himself beyond the camaraderie she normally shared with men. Sunny wasn't certain what had happened between them, but she knew the memory of dark gray eyes had come to her mind time and again. Recently a detailed memory of the man flashed through her mind with increasing frequency. The odd thing was that the contact had been brief, but the memory endured.

Almost absently Sunny returned to their conversation, but her teasing tone had vanished. "When I do settle down, it's going to be with a gentle, even-tempered man who doesn't chase everything in skirts."

Surprised, Mike momentarily jerked his gaze from the heavy traffic to glance at his partner. He ignored the stab at his life-style. There had been a subtle change in Sunny lately, but he hadn't been able put his finger on what it was. Now he had a hint—maybe more than a hint.

Mike had known Sunny for several years, and their friendship stood them in good stead as partners. They knew each other well enough that they could often anticipate each other as they worked together. He couldn't have asked for a better partner—or a more striking one. Except for her slightly upturned nose and the sprinkling of freckles across it, she would have been considered extraordinarily beautiful. He was the envy of every guy at the station.

Even though he'd noticed a bit of the sparkle had gone out of her eyes and her enthusiasm for life had dimmed a bit, Mike had never had a hint of anything like *this*—that she would ever consider marriage. Everyone knew she was married to her career.

"Are my ears failing me? What do you mean 'settle down'? You won't give any man a second glance. I didn't think you knew the male species existed—with the exception of me, of course. When was the last time you had a date?"

"Well, you took me to dinner last week, or don't you count?"

"No. Going dutch doesn't count, Sun."

Regretting the slip of her tongue, she crossed her arms across her chest. She'd had no intention of revealing her dreams. Settling down. The cottage with the white picket fence. A man with whom she could share her life. A child who would be the ultimate expression of their love.

That far-reaching dream had monopolized her mind recently. Gradually this idea had emerged from her growing dissatisfaction with her life. Seeking another goal, a greater challenge, she'd switched from trauma-team nurse to paramedic, which daily demanded her utmost both physically and emotionally. But the change had not averted the restlessness. The feeling had only increased, and poked holes in her usual contentment.

The driving force that had kept her life totally centered on her career for so many years had shifted. Perhaps her upcoming birthday had focused her thoughts on her personal life. She had loads of friends, even a few close friends like Mike, but there was a vacancy in her heart she intended to fill. She couldn't blame her restlessness on turning thirty—she knew the change had been gradual. If she was honest with herself, Sunny could pinpoint the day the change had begun.

Although Mike *was* her best friend, she hadn't meant for that thought to escape the privacy of her heart—not yet anyway.

"Egads," Sunny muttered as they arrived at the scene of the accident. Her frown deepened as the siren groaned into silence.

Mike maneuvered the emergency unit a little closer to the intersection as an officer waved them through. More than a dozen lanes of traffic merged at this intersection, but now the cars stood motionless in all directions. The same could not be said for the drivers' tempers—blaring and beeping horns interrupted the hum of idling engines. Visible waves of heat and exhaust hovered above the black pavement.

Tossing her sunglasses on the dash, Sunny opened her door and jumped to the ground, grabbing her equipment from the side panel.

"You check out the Bronco, I'll see to the sedan," Mike shouted over the hood of the truck as he started toward the glass-strewn intersection and the woman who stood crying beside the crinkled hood of her car.

Hurrying toward the Bronco, Sunny surveyed the damage. The sedan had most likely run a red light and hit the Bronco broadside. An officer stood beside the Ford, copying information onto his clipboard as he spoke with the man still seated inside. It wasn't likely the driver was seriously injured if he was already giving a report.

Sunny crossed in front of the car and quickly nodded to the officer. Ignoring the officer's wink and appreciative once-over, she turned her attention to the man in the Bronco.

"Sir? Are you experiencing any pain?" Her eyes narrowed against the sun as she clinically appraised what she could see of the chiseled masculine face through the open window. His sunglasses hid his eyes. A vague sense of familiarity streaked through her mind. She quickly dismissed the idea.

"Sir?" Sunny repeated as she noted the pallor under the deeply tanned complexion. The man's respirations were a little rapid, but that could be expected under the circumstances.

"I'm fine," he growled without glancing at her. His gaze was fixed on her partner, who stood a few feet away.

"Why don't I check you out, just to make certain?" Sunny suggested as she reached for the door handle.

The door flew open, and Sunny jumped back to avoid being hit. Since people often didn't realize they'd been hurt or were in shock, she watched him as he stepped from the truck.

Black jeans worn to a soft charcoal gray were tucked into black boots that had seen better days. The white cotton of his shirt was pulled taut across his chest. As he stood on the pavement, Sunny was aware of his height—something that didn't usually strike her with her own five feet eight inches. He stood still, stiff, his hand clenched white around the window frame.

Reluctantly Drew looked at the paramedic who stood on the other side of the door. Strawberry blond. He'd only known one person with that exact color hair— strawberry blond. He couldn't have been more stunned if he'd been slugged in the solar plexus. He couldn't force air either into or out of his lungs. It had been years ago, but he was transported back to the emergency room as if it were yesterday. Even in the ninety-degree heat of this afternoon, he could remember the chills that had racked his body.

Air finally swooshed from his chest as he returned

to reality. Damn! Soft brown eyes—the very same eyes that had offered him sanity when he'd thought his had deserted him. The harsh, haunting memories swept over him like a tidal wave. Memories he'd forced aside almost daily. Memories that often yanked him from a deep sleep.

Yet Drew never thought of that life-shattering day without the image of this woman slipping into his mind and somehow softening the repercussions of what had happened. After he'd heard the prognosis from the surgeon, he'd refused to see her. He'd never expected to see her again. Expressionless, he stared.

Her appearance here today churned up his anger and bitterness. He'd believed those feelings were part of the past. He forced his stare from her face to the name tag, which read "Sunny Steele." He'd never asked her name. Sunny—somehow the name fit.

Oh, he'd heard that name often enough to be sick of it. He glowered at the name tag. Damn! At times the world was too small—Sunny, his brother's partner. Drew had decided no one could live up to the praises his brother had sung about her. He'd been wrong.

No, her sudden appearance today could never make a difference. Many things had been decided in the arroyo that rainy day. He'd forfeited almost everything important to him for the life of a teenager. He now faced life as a cripple—oh yeah, he knew the appropriate word was *handicapped*, but on days like today, only "cripple" seemed to express his feelings.

It had cost him his career. There wasn't a day he didn't long to be out in the field again, doing what he did best—what he *used* to do best, he corrected himself. He'd achieved an unblemished reputation in undercover work. He'd never forget the Granger case. It had been one of the last cases he'd been assigned, and if it hadn't been for the agility of his body and mind, he knew he would never have lived to tell about it. Never lived to pull that boy from the arroyo. He knew he would make the same sacrifice again, even knowing the cost. But today he once again understood just how far-reaching the effects of the accident had been. He no longer saw himself as a whole person.

"Go find someone else to *check out.*"

Sunny watched as the man quietly shut the door of the Bronco, his body brushing past her. His verbal attack had felt almost personal. She frowned. As the man started toward Mike, she saw he was limping.

"Sir, you *are* hurt. You're limping."

"I'm quite aware of that fact," he hollered over his shoulder as he continued to limp.

"You've been injured. Let me look at your leg. It could be serious." She felt ridiculous, but she kept trailing the man. Maybe he simply didn't care for female paramedics. Maybe he would let Mike help him.

Mike snapped the equipment box shut. He felt relieved the woman hadn't been injured; the seat belt had saved her. He'd check on Sunny—maybe that order of onion rings wasn't so far off after all. Stunned, Mike jerked his head back. His thoughts halted abruptly as he recognized his brother walking toward him, and Sunny hurrying along behind him.

"Mike, this man is hurt. He's limping, but he won't let me look at his leg," Sunny said as she set the heavy equipment box on the street.

"Sunny," Mike interrupted as he put out his hand to stop her from saying more.

"That fool ran the red light and hit me broadside. I saw her coming and tried to swerve out of the way, but she was driving like a maniac."

Mike frowned. "Are you okay?"

Glancing back toward the Bronco, Drew answered, "Hell, no! I just picked up the new Bronco for the ranch not thirty minutes ago, and look at it now."

"Mike," Sunny persisted, "this man is injured."

Drew turned on Sunny and whipped off his sunglasses and glared at her with dark gray eyes. "Back off. I'm not hurt. I'm a cripple."

Sunny mutely stared at him. The lieutenant. Her breath caught in her throat as the familiarity she'd felt a few minutes ago slid into place. Just as quickly she wanted to reject the thought. Impossible. Her gaze darted away and then back to the man standing defiantly before her. His hands anchored on his narrow waist. His look challenged Sunny. But to what? She had no idea.

This was a first. Mike had never seen Sunny so pale, not even in the worst of circumstances. He glanced between the two. His gregarious partner at a loss for words? Squeezing her shoulder, Mike made the necessary introductions. "Sunny, meet Drew, my brother. Drew, this is my partner, Sunny."

"Your brother?" Sunny felt her face heat with color. Questions flooded her mind. Lieutenant? A cripple? He offered the briefest possible nod in acknowledgment of their introduction. She watched his gray eyes darken as they pinned her, challenged her, and stripped her of her customary confidence.

Her mind wanted to call him a four-letter word. Her heart wrenched in confusion.

Even though the heavy noontime traffic had begun to move around the disabled vehicles, the rushing roar in her ears blocked out all sound. Sunny looked from one man to the other. A tangle of facts, of questions, of feelings, whirled through her mind and tumbled pell-mell into her heart, rendering her speechless.

Drew watched the length of Sunny's hair swing back and forth in rhythm as she glanced from him to Mike and back to him. Surprise. Disbelief. He inventoried the expressions that raced across her face. Was she that shocked he was handicapped?

Drew looked at the crumpled side of his new truck.

With the ease of practice, he mentally detached himself from the piquant beauty whom his brother had often spoken of in glowing terms. When he heard Mike speak quietly to Sunny, he turned back to the pair standing opposite him. A frown furrowed his forehead. Exactly what was their relationship?

Mike looked at his brother as his hand fell from Sunny's shoulder. He'd thought sparks might fly if he ever succeeded in introducing the two of them, but this confrontation was more like a smoldering fire. No, that wasn't it either, but there was something happening here he didn't understand.

Glancing at her partner, Sunny took a deep breath of the exhaust-filled air, picked up her equipment, and retreated to the emergency vehicle. She wanted to run, but her pride and the heavy equipment she carried prevented it.

Mike observed Sunny's retreat. "Hot damn. Didn't I tell you she was magnificent?"

Drew didn't answer but turned to watch. Once again she wore a uniform—not the loose-hanging scrubs of last time but a dark-colored, curve-hugging uniform of slacks and shirt.

"I've been trying to talk her into coming up to the ranch with me on Friday. We have four days off."

"You can forget that! Don't bring her to the ranch."

"What's that supposed to mean?"

"Exactly what it sounds like."

"An order, Drew?"

"Take it however you want, but just don't bring her—ever." As Sunny disappeared around the side of the truck, Drew admitted the obvious. From a distance, she was absolutely lovely. Up close she was lethal.

Her gaze glued to the man who stood beside her partner, Sunny sat in the hot truck and ignored the paperwork that was a constant part of this job. The lieutenant. Andrew Williams. Mike's brother. She slipped on her sunglasses, feeling the need for the protection of the reflective lenses. The tight set of her shoulders relaxed a little as her tension eased.

What had happened out there? She shook her head in disbelief. Seeing his eyes, the very ones she'd dreamed of even last night, had really thrown her. She wasn't used to being caught by surprise.

With a couple of deep breaths, Sunny's calm returned. She sifted through what Mike had told her about his older brother. Mike admired him. They were close. She knew he lived on a ranch near Santa Fe that she recalled had something to do with horses. He had boys—foster kids? Mike had never said too much about them. She did know he wasn't married.

His handicap . . . He called himself a cripple. She grimaced at the word. She would never have connected him with the man in the hospital. His face had been battered and swollen. His attitude was different then, too. He sounded bitter now, almost cynical. This man needed no one! But his eyes—she'd never forgotten the striking color. And the magnetic pull remained.

It was indeed a small world—or was it? Now that Sunny thought about it, she didn't think he'd even recognized her, and why would he? No one would remember a particular nurse under the extreme pain he'd been experiencing.

Drew and Mike seemed unaware they were standing in the middle of the intersection, but she didn't think they were oblivious to her. As they looked in her direction, she had the distinct feeling she was the topic of discussion.

She couldn't resist contrasting the two. Mike was as fair as his brother was dark, and Drew towered over his brother. Although Sunny knew only five years separated them, life had imprinted character lines on Drew's face stating he'd lived far beyond his thirty-four years. There was a toughness about him—a touch of mystery that intrigued Sunny. Was it that same quality that had initiated her preoccupation? Somehow the expression in his eyes had pulled her into its vortex, and she'd never been free of it.

Sunny watched in surprise as Mike grabbed his brother and gave him a bear hug followed by a forceful slap on the back. When Mike started toward the truck, she suddenly found the dreaded paperwork of utmost interest.

Mike looked at Sunny as he fastened his seat belt and started the engine. Her face was shielded by the fall of her hair, and she didn't look up from her work as he spoke into the radio and pulled away from the intersection.

Sunny looked out the window. A slow smile encompassed her face. "That man is a boar. Not a bore—I doubt he could ever be that." Sunny cleared the funny little catch in her throat. "I'm talking b-o-a-r." She spelled out the word as Mike pulled into the traffic. "One of those oversize snapping, snarling pigs." Sunny chuckled at her own joke.

With effort, Mike kept a straight face as he asked, "My brother? Is that who you're talking about, Sun?"

"Cool it, Mike. I've never felt like such an idiot in my entire life. Why didn't you tell me your brother was—"

"Handicapped?" Mike interrupted. "His accident was so long ago, and he rarely limps anymore. I never think of Drew in that way. It's just that he hit his leg on impact in the accident and probably bruised the old injury."

"No, Mike. 'Handicapped' is the last word I would ever use to describe your brother." The impact Drew had made on her years before was still part of her, and today the effect had been different but just as powerful.

Sunny started again, hoping Mike hadn't picked up on her lapse. "What I started to ask, Mike, was why didn't you tell me your brother was . . ." Sunny blushed. "Never mind." After a moment she added, "If he didn't frown all the time, he might be good-looking."

Mike's eyebrows raised in question. "Tell me, Sunny, why do all females think he's so good-looking? I'm the handsome one."

"Yes, and with an ego to match. But your brother, well, he's different in that rough, dark sort of way."

"So you're finally intrigued."

"What are you talking about?" When Mike didn't answer, Sunny questioned him, "Does he have something against the female population, or is it just me?" But before Mike could answer, she continued, "I've only seen gray eyes like his one other time. . . ."

A secret smile hovered as Mike sucked in his cheeks to keep from smiling outright. "His eyes turn almost black when he gets riled."

"What are you grinning about? You look like the cat who swallowed the canary."

"Not a thing, Sunny. I feel good. Don't you? No one was injured. Lunch is just a few blocks away."

"I don't think I'm very hungry anymore." Sunny surprised herself with the unheard-of idea.

"You? Not hungry?" Mike hooted in disbelief even as he made a mental note of Sunny's odd behavior.

"What in the world is so funny, Mike?"

"You wouldn't believe it if I told you. By the way, I promised Drew I'd pick him up at the garage as soon as our shift is over. I'll drop you off after that."

Of all days, why had her car decided to go on the fritz today?

TWO

"Damn!" Drew muttered as he watched Mike's car come to a stop beside him. Couldn't his brother go anywhere without her? What was he supposed to do? Climb over her and sit in the back seat? No, she was squeezing into the back—and she'd changed into shorts.

Just as Drew sat on the front seat, Sunny screeched. He glanced back and saw her pelvis tilted toward the sky.

"Mike, do you have anything I can put under me? This seat is too hot to sit on."

Before Mike could answer, Drew advised, "If you'd wear modest clothing, that wouldn't happen."

"Modest? Did you say *modest*?"

Mike chuckled and said, "I'll find something in the trunk to cover the seat."

"Never mind."

"You sure?"

"Yes. Let's get out of here."

As she removed her hands from under her legs, she realized the seat was tolerable now. When she glanced up, Drew was facing straight ahead. Sunny tried to ignore the magnetism of his broad shoulders and the dark hair brushing his collar. In the rearview mirror,

28

Mike smiled and gave her a quick wink before he pulled into the traffic.

Normally Sunny got along with everyone. She knew there had been a special rapport between her and Drew when he'd been in the hospital. But today things had changed. He could rankle her with just a few words as no one else ever had. And why did Mike seem to get such a kick out of it?

These two were a pair she could do without!

Thirty years old today! Sunny stood in front of the mirrored closet doors in her bedroom, pivoting in the lace teddy. Sheer panty hose covered her long legs. She'd hated her skinny legs during her coltish years, but now she knew they fit her body perfectly. Not bad for thirty; not lush and beautiful, but slender and certainly healthy. She kept her body fit. No matter what the weather, she jogged at least ten to twelve miles a week.

Her expression in the mirror sobered as her hands settled on her waist. What would it feel like to have a man's hands touching her? Hers was a body untouched. Not one person, probably not even her father, would believe she was still a virgin on her thirtieth birthday. Until recently she'd never given it a thought. She'd never had the time or the inclination to have an affair. Now, when she did consider the situation, her virginity felt decidedly awkward.

How could one special day feel so topsy-turvy? She'd rushed through life during her twenties, pursuing her goals with a tenacity that left her with neither time nor interest for anything else.

In reaching each of her goals—most on time, others ahead of schedule—she'd understood her strengths, she'd tapped them, and she'd become a success. She loved her life, but she was now ready to find the missing piece to fill the vacant spot her demanding career could not fill.

Friends claimed turning thirty was devastating. She didn't feel that way; she simply felt as though she needed to take a few days off to assimilate her feelings . . . her thoughts . . . her plans. A quietness had developed within Sunny that felt different—good. The hard-driving, goal-oriented person had taken a backseat to her deepest thoughts and feelings. She needed time to plan—to initiate her new goal, which was totally unlike any other she'd ever set for herself.

Pulling a mint green silk dress from an antique chifforobe, she took it from a padded hanger and slipped into it. There was a knock at her bedroom door.

"You about ready, honey?"

Sunny smiled. Her father was as impatient as ever. Their reservations weren't for another hour. "I'll meet you downstairs in about twenty minutes, Dad."

Sunny took his muffled grumble as an assent and finished dressing. He was leaving soon for an extended trip to Australia. He meant the world to her. She'd almost lost him to a heart attack when she was sixteen. That day had drastically changed her life, and it had given her the impetus to achieve goal after goal, but she'd never felt the need to get her own place.

Pulling the brush through her thick hair one last time, Sunny put on a smile that didn't feel too genuine before going downstairs to meet her father.

The popular restaurant was crowded as usual on this Friday night. Even though they had reservations, she'd expected to wait. But after a short murmur to the maître d', they were escorted through a maze of diners to a door at the rear.

Joe Steele stopped in front of a closed door, thanking the man and glancing at his watch at the same time. Quickly and quietly he pulled Sunny into his arms and kissed her cheek. "Happy Birthday, my little sunshine." As he opened the door, the roar of *"Surprise!"*

echoed throughout the restaurant. At least fifty people, some in uniform with radios on their belts, stood around the lavishly decorated room, enjoying her utter shock.

Her father's booming voice rang out, "You only turn thirty once, Sunny." With his announcement, chorused greetings and catcalls emitted from the males of the party.

By anyone's standards, the celebration was a huge success. Friends whom she hadn't seen in months were there. A live band played, champagne bubbled freely, and the gourmet dinner was prepared to perfection. What more could a person want? Sunny quizzed herself. She knew the answer. It was simply a matter of the most efficient way to accomplish it.

Pleading a need for rest, Sunny sat down. She had danced with every man in the room at least once. A tiered birthday cake, decorated with miniature ambulance and medical supplies, was rolled in, and everyone began to sing. With a realization that was heart-stopping, Sunny blew at the candles. Others only saw her in terms of her career. Did her father see her that way, too? They were right. The realization that her life was one-dimensional was reinforced tonight. She'd heard several of her friends mention to her father that no one was more dedicated than Sunny. Well, they were all in for a surprise.

By the looks of today, Sunny decided, summer was behind them, and changeable fall weather was here. A sheet of dirty water washed down over the truck, obscuring their vision. Sunny felt Mike ease off the accelerator.

In the space of a day the temperature had fallen twenty degrees, from Indian summer to chilly gray fall. Sunny could see neither the Sandia Mountains to the east nor Nine Mile Hill to the west. Her uniform was damp, clinging like wet spaghetti to the sides of a cold pan. The rain had begun before dawn this morning.

The moisture was needed, but the side effects could be devastating.

They were running low on supplies. Low on morale, too, Sunny admitted to herself. This last week a heart attack victim they'd worked feverishly over had died, and a seven-year-old girl had lost her eyesight playing with her brother's chemistry set. In this line of work you had to take the bad with the good. Sunny loved her job and she knew she was good, very good, at what she did. She had reminded herself of this over and over in the weeks since her birthday, but the deep restlessness played havoc with her usual peace of mind.

Uncomfortable with the feeling that was becoming too familiar, she'd even gone so far as to ask for a week of vacation. It had been denied due to a shortage of manpower. Sunny wanted to talk about it with someone. But who? Mike was the logical person, but she didn't know if he would understand. It was time to set a definite time to begin to execute her plan. But she would need a few days to shop for everything she would require before beginning her new adventure, and so far she hadn't been able to get any extra time off.

The signal light a half block away flashed yellow. "Great, just what we need," Mike muttered. "Another delay." Mike glanced over at Sunny. Unaware they had stopped, she stared off into space, not seeing the gloomy outside world, only her own world, which, if her expression told anything, wasn't much brighter. She hadn't told him, but he'd heard she'd asked for extra days off. Usually Sunny was very open, but this was different, Sunny was different—not really depressed but withdrawn. "Why don't you tell me about it, Sunny?" Mike asked.

"Tell you what?" Sunny asked as she continued to look out the window.

"To put it delicately, your lack of enthusiasm for life lately . . . for the last several weeks, in fact." When Sunny didn't acknowledge she'd even heard him, he asked, "Does it have anything to do with turning thirty?"

"Yes. Well . . . kind of."

Mike was surprised by her ready but almost inaudible answer. This might be easier than he'd expected, but Mike's attention was diverted when a blaring horn sounded.

Traffic began to creep along at a snail's pace. Street-wide rivers of muddy water rushed down the pavement and flowed over the curbs. When the rain came down for this long and this hard, the normally adequate drainage system could not keep up.

Sunny's thoughts flew back to the present as they crossed the Embudo Arroyo. It was running a good six feet high. All the concrete ditches were filled due to the runoff from the Sandias. She and Mike had received special training in rescue operations for arroyos, but Mike always got antsy when the arroyos were running as they were today. Now she understood why—Drew. Sunny knew what danger the concrete ditches held; she'd seen several victims who had been thrashed about by the rushing wall of water. One of whom was Mike's brother. The lieutenant now called himself a "cripple" because of it.

Thunderstorms in the mountains could cause a flash flood and catch a person unawares. Often rescue workers risked their own lives to save someone who had disregarded the safety rules. Anyone who was in the paramedic business understood that danger was often an integral part of the job.

Mike's frustration level peaked as another sheet of water was thrown onto their windshield by a truck in the next lane. "I'm wet and hungry. Hell, I'm exhausted." He glanced over at Sunny. "You don't look too good yourself." Mike's voice trailed off in disgust before he added, "Thank goodness there's only another hour on this shift. I'm going home and fix a huge pot of chili and let it simmer in the crock pot while I catch up on a couple hours of well-deserved sleep."

"Everything will look better in the morning," Sunny answered.

Mike grunted, then asked, "What are you doing this evening? Do you want to share dinner? You bring the wine and tortillas, then you won't have to cook."

"Chili sounds great."

The sound of the doorbell jerked Mike from a deep sleep. He'd set his alarm; Sunny must be early. He sniffed appreciatively; the chili smelled perfect. As the doorbell rang again, he stretched and yawned. Rolling out of bed, he pulled on his jeans, not bothering to button them.

He opened the door as the bell rang the third time.

"Oh, Drew." Another yawn stretched out Mike's sentence. "What a surprise!"

"You didn't get my message," Drew stated.

"Hi, Uncle Mike. What's for dinner? It sure smells great," the precocious nine-year-old Rico stated matter-of-factly as he headed toward the kitchen. "I'm starved."

Mike glanced toward the kitchen, then at his brother. "Come on in. I take it you're here for dinner? For once, you're in luck."

"I left a message at the station."

Before Drew could go on, Rico piped up, "Drew's my dad now, and you really are my uncle. Should I call him Dad or Drew?"

Drew grinned. "The adoption hearing was today. But I need to stay over to sign the final papers tomorrow. I thought maybe Rico and I could camp out in your living room since the weather is so bad. I hate driving to Santa Fe just to turn around and come right back in the morning."

"Sorry. I forgot all about the hearing. This has been a hell of a week. Everything went okay? Is he officially yours?"

Before Drew could do more than nod, the doorbell

rang again. "That'll be Sunny. Get the door, Drew. I'll check on dinner."

"Sunny," Drew muttered under his breath. "Damn!"

Sunny's smile drooped as the door opened. Her eyes narrowed, her thoughts raced. Her gaze dropped from his face. All dressed up, too. A pin-striped charcoal suit, a pearl gray shirt, and a burgundy tie. She glanced down at her own attire—old jeans that fit more than a tad too snugly, and a baggy sweatshirt exclaiming the superiority of woman. She wanted to hide behind the nearby shrubbery. Instead she lifted her chin a notch and flashed her best smile.

Sunny watched Drew's immediate reaction—his eyes darkened to almost black.

"Let Sunny in out of the rain."

Drew stepped back, allowing her entrance before quietly closing the door. He turned toward the pair. "For God's sake, Mike, button your jeans and put on a shirt."

Mike ignored his brother's command as he swept Sunny into an embrace, the wine and tortillas smashed between her and Mike's bare chest. Sunny's dripping umbrella teetered above them as Mike kissed her loudly on the lips.

When Sunny could extricate herself from Mike's stranglehold, she whispered, "I don't know what you're up to, but stuff it."

In a lightning-quick decision she added aloud, "Something's come up and I'm not going to be able to stay. Here's your wine and the tortillas you requested. Have a delightful dinner."

"Shut the door, Drew. She's staying."

The door clicked shut, and she watched Drew walk past them toward the kitchen.

Wrestling the umbrella from her, Mike hung it on the coat tree as he spoke. "Whoa there, Sunny. What's the problem? Afraid you'll lose another battle of the wills with my brother if you stick around?'' Mike spoke in a feigned whisper as his gaze probed her expression, looking for a hint of the usual Sunny.

A glance toward the kitchen confirmed her suspicions. Drew stood in the doorway. A small boy stood quietly beside him, his hand clasped in Drew's. Sunny's eyes softened and her shoulders lost their stiffness as she looked at the young child. New jeans were tucked into shiny brown cowboy boots. A brown and blue plaid shirt half-stuffed into his jeans gave him a lopsided look. Sunny's eyes sparkled as she smiled at the boy.

Drew frowned as she smiled at his son.

"Is she your girlfriend, Uncle Mike? I saw you kiss her, just like in the movies. Yuck!"

Hugging Sunny close to his side, Mike answered, "This is Sunny, Rico. Rico's a member of our family as of today. We're going to have a celebration party. Right, Rico?"

"Right, Uncle Mike." Rico's smile flashed a bright white against his toasty brown skin.

"And you remember my brother, Drew. Don't you, Sunny?"

When no one answered, Mike walked through the archway to the kitchen, whistling and pulling Sunny along in his wake.

"I'll leave my contribution to your party and be on my way. It sounds as if this is family stuff. I wouldn't think of intruding." Sunny's voice sounded hollow even to her own ears.

"Don't leave on my account."

Sunny spun around. He could speak in a somewhat civil tone, after all. Her gaze touched on Drew but quickly darted to Mike. The efficiency kitchen seemed smaller than usual.

"I really can't stay."

"Nonsense. You can and you will," Mike inserted quickly.

Immediately Sunny's assertive, independent spirit took over, but before she could object, Mike continued, "I made the chili just the way you like it. Besides that, I want you to stay."

Drew cleared his throat. "It seems as though Rico and I are the intruders. I didn't realize you two had a date. We can go out for dinner. We wouldn't want to infringe on your privacy."

Privacy? Did he believe she and Mike were a couple?

Before the conversation could get out of control, Mike said, "We're all adults. Can't we share a simple meal together?"

"I'm not an adult, Uncle Mike. I'm just nine, but the judge did say I was mature, huh, Dad?"

"Dad? That sounds great. Congratulations." Mike slapped Drew on the shoulder as he pumped his hand.

Sunny looked at the two men and the young boy whose eyes worshiped them both. She didn't understand all of this talk, but this was definitely a family night.

Rico said to Sunny, "I want you to celebrate with us, Sunny. I have a new dad." The young boy swallowed. "My other dad was killed in the line of duty." He glanced at Drew. "Right?"

"You're absolutely right, son. Your dad was a great cop—one of the best."

"They gave me the flag that was over his . . . I'm going to keep it forever. And I'm going to be a cop someday, too. Just like both my dads."

The young boy had a fragility about him that tugged at Sunny's heart. She blinked back the tears. "You should be very proud. I'd be honored to help you celebrate. Thanks for including me."

"Have a seat, Sunny," Mike ordered. "I'll set the table, and we'll be ready in no time."

"I'll pull my own weight and set the table for you."

Laughing, Mike gave her figure the once-over.

"How much do you weigh? I'd guess about one fifteen. Wouldn't you, Drew?"

"You're going to get it for this, Mr. Macho. I've had enough of your clown act. Why don't you go join the circus?"

"What's he going to get? Don't you like my Uncle Mike?"

Sunny groaned, but with one glance at Rico's worried brown eyes, her irritation vanished. She would ignore the supposed adults in this situation and get acquainted with Rico.

"I like your uncle just fine . . . at least most of the time." She glanced at her friend and shook her head at Mike's exaggerated wink. "Rico, why don't you help me set the table, and then we can see if his chili is as good as he claims?"

Drew turned and went into the living room to slip out of his suit jacket. Again he wondered what the relationship was between Sunny and Mike. On the heels of that thought, he reminded himself it made no difference to him anyway. But instead of sitting down on the couch to read the paper as he'd planned, he found himself once again standing in the archway between the two rooms, watching.

Sunny obviously knew her way around Mike's kitchen. Drew frowned. He wanted to dislike her. He needed an excuse to put her from his mind permanently, but her genuine, unaffected delight in his son touched an unprotected spot deep within him.

Dinner proved to be interesting. Sunny had little to say but a lot to listen to. Drew and Rico filled Mike in on the details of Rico's adoption. Refusing even a second glass of wine, Sunny sat quietly watching the three converse about family and the ranch, reminiscing about special memories. She didn't really hear all of the words, just the tone of contentment, the mood of acceptance, of love.

"Dad, tell Sunny about the time you rescued Jesse from the—" Before Rico could finish the sentence, a quick shake of Drew's head silenced the boy.

She didn't think Drew had glanced her way one time during the meal. It was time to go home. Sunny excused herself and called a cab.

Sunny stood in the archway for a moment before Mike glanced up and saw her. "I'll say good night. Thanks for dinner, Mike. It was delicious."

"It's not even nine yet."

"I know, but I think this week has taken more out of me than I realized. I've called a cab. It should be here any time."

"I could have driven you home."

"I know, but thanks anyway. Your chili was the best, as usual." Reaching up to hug Mike, she brushed her lips across his cheek. She caught the scowl of his brother over Mike's shoulder.

It continued to rain, but softly now. The cab driver wasn't pushing his philosophy of life on her as the one who'd brought her to Mike's had, and she was glad. She needed time to think.

She didn't understand Mike's brother at all. He seemed unaware of her, and when he did deign to look at her, it was always with a frown. It was as if he had cataloged her assets and she'd come up grossly lacking. She couldn't understand this since she'd never had trouble making friends before. Matter of fact, she'd never known anyone who had treated her with such obvious disdain.

He was better-looking than she'd imagined. He had a flash of smile that could turn any girl's heart, but it hadn't been directed at her—only at Mike and Rico. And when he talked with Rico, she saw gentleness and understanding. But that was the only time she'd seen a glimpse of the man she'd known in the hospital.

His limp! He'd said he was a cripple. Sunny searched

her memory for a moment. She was certain he hadn't
limped tonight. So why would he call himself a cripple?

Rico was asleep on the floor in the living room when
Drew came into the kitchen. Mike was finishing the
dishes.

"She's some kind of lady." When Drew didn't answer, he continued, "She's nearly perfect in my
estimation."

"As I recall, you're not always particularly selective."

"What's with you and Sunny, anyway? You both try
to act as if the other one doesn't exist. You barely
speak to each other."

When his brother didn't answer, Mike continued, "Did
I tell you about her birthday party? Her dad and I planned
it. We surprised her, too. She turned thirty. Can you
believe that? She doesn't look thirty, do you think?
There's a lot of woman packed into that slender body."

"Humph."

"She's never given any man the time of day. Her
career has been her life. Every man I know has tried to
date her, myself included, but no one has succeeded. But
now . . . now I think she's interested. I doubt she'll date
very many men, though. She's the marrying type."

Drew crossed his arms over his chest, deep in
thought. His chair was balanced on two legs, his feet
propped on the edge of the kitchen table. Thank God
he and Rico had interrupted tonight after all. Did Sunny
have her sights set on Mike?

He'd always prided himself on being a fair and logical person, but he would never be able to handle having
Sunny as part of their family. Never.

THREE

She was on a high. Flying. Invincible. The soft rain-drops pelted gently against Sunny's uplifted face, cascaded down the long column of her neck, dipping under the faded T-shirt boasting ''Duke City Marathon'' to find sanctuary in the cotton sports bra that held her breasts firmly as she ran.

The German shepherd matched her long-gaited pace. His dark coat occasionally brushed his mistress's bare thigh as if to remind her of his presence. The two ran with the fluid grace of a single dancer, as though they were linked by a primal rhythm.

The dark clouds that had burst earlier over the Sandia Mountains now gently showered the city. Sunny breathed deeply of the fresh scent. The rain cooled her flushed, perspiring body. Two more miles to go. She was aware of herself as a woman as never before. She felt in tune with her body, with her heart.

The inner reflections and the ensuing conclusions of the past three days had settled into a deep harmony in her soul. Goal-oriented as always, she had resolved to be married within the year—before she turned thirty-one. Her philosophy had always been that if you wanted something—or in this case someone—you should go after what you wanted.

A dreamy smile pulled up the corners of her mouth. The tip of her tongue tasted the saltiness of her perspiration mixed with rain. There were boxes of new clothing sitting on her bed at home. It was money well spent. There was only one thing left to do—a new hairstyle. In a couple of hours she had an appointment with a stylist. But she would be all dressed up with no place to go if she didn't figure out a way to meet Mr. Right.

She ran, only partially aware of her surroundings, trusting the two-year-old Prince Charming, who was aware of everything around them. He was a highly trained police dog. Her father had given him to her when he'd been thrown out of the police program due to the dog's problem with motion sickness. Without a shadow of a doubt, Sunny knew he would protect her with his life.

Her daydreams faded with a sharp bark from Prince. A police car, lights flashing, was parked beside the Embudo Channel. A small crowd had gathered, with everyone looking up the arroyo. Her brain suddenly clicked at the sound of rushing water.

Chest heaving, Sunny slowed as she reached the bridge crossing. A low growl rumbled from the dog as she stood running in place. An officer she'd worked with before pulled ropes from the trunk of his car.

"What's up?" she asked in a breathy voice, her body bobbing with the in-place jog.

"Get back, please; we're busy," a young officer answered.

A rookie, she thought. "John, it's me, Sunny. Can I help?"

The officer pulled his head out of the trunk, his arms full of heavy rope, his gaze flicking over her. "I didn't recognize you, Sunny."

He handed the rope to his partner, shed his jacket,

and pulled a life vest from the trunk. "We've got a young child in the arroyo. Gotta get a rope across here, fast, before he gets any further down the channel. We're the last chance he has. The rescue unit is coming, but there's no time to wait."

"Give me the other vest," Sunny said. Breathing hard, she continued to walk in place, trying to keep the leg cramps at bay.

John flicked his eyes between his new partner and Sunny, betting he'd have a better chance with Sunny. Handing her the vest, he looked at her. "No net. Nothing but this rope, Sunny."

Sunny nodded, understanding.

"What about your dog?"

"He's trained for police work, so he'll be fine." Pulling her T-shirt out of the nylon running shorts, she wiped her face before she slipped into the life jacket and fastened it with care.

At the edge of the concrete embankment, Sunny patted the dog's head and gave the firm command, "Stay."

Carefully climbing down the steep slope of the metal ladder cemented into the side of the concrete-lined ditch, she heard Prince's low growl of concern. Not taking her eyes from her task, she shouted over the roar of the water. "It's okay, boy. Stay."

People lined the well-worn path beside the arroyo, shouting and pointing, but Sunny heard only the roar of the rushing water.

Adrenaline surged through her body. Fear clutched at her empty stomach. She glanced down at the water, which propelled debris along its tumbling path. She estimated the water to be moving at least twenty—no, more likely thirty—miles an hour. How deep? She didn't want to know.

Sunny carefully tied the rope onto the metal that was embedded in the concrete, double-checking it—at least three lives could depend upon it. Coiling the rope, she threw it with all her strength to the other side. If she missed, there might not be time to try again.

Sunny blanked the fear from her mind, filling it with the facts she remembered from her training. In her peripheral vision, she could see the excited crowd pointing as a yellow object came into view and disappeared just as suddenly.

In the background, she could hear the siren growing louder. She prayed they'd get here in time to help. Could the child even still be alive, let alone able to grab a rope? She swallowed the bile that threatened. The ache in her midsection tightened, making a deep breath impossible.

Sunny had a bad feeling about this. There was always talk about arroyo rescues, none of it encouraging. Many times heroics were necessary to rescue someone. Her mind switched to scenes in the ER—battered bodies. Drew! Had he felt this stark terror?

This was her first experience in this kind of rushing water. She was a strong swimmer, but that wouldn't help much in this raging current. She was not properly clothed, and her legs were already cramping from not cooling down after her run. But, no matter what she felt physically or mentally, she'd do whatever she needed to do in order to save this child.

Glancing across the dirty river of water, she nodded to the officer that she was ready.

Her shoes lost their grip on the slippery wall of the channel, and Sunny slid into the edge of the current. She heard Prince's piercing bark over the roar of the water. The water felt frigid against her bare legs, sending a cold shiver up her damp spine. Her shoulders tensed as the cold invaded her limbs.

The child's head surfaced again amid the floating debris. He was in the middle of the arroyo. She would not be able to reach him from where she presently stood. Sunny heard the bystanders screaming to the child to grab the rope, but she knew his chances were slim—he would probably go under it.

Even as she heard the rescue unit screech to a stop above her, Sunny grabbed a little of the slack in the rope and wrapped it around her wrist and across the palm of her hand. She stepped into the dark water. She would have to try to stop the child with her own body so he wouldn't go under the rope.

With a death grip, Sunny held the rope in her left hand. She reached with her right hand toward the middle of the arroyo. She still wouldn't be able to reach the child. Another shiver shook her. The current pushed against her upper thighs. She moved farther into the current. She prayed she'd find a "dead spot" where the current wouldn't be quite so strong.

Her breath came in painful, choppy gasps. She clenched her chattering teeth. The water was up to her waist now. Facts about rescue clicked in her brain, but fear fought for supremacy. She would need to grasp more than the yellow material of the child's jacket—it would simply tear off the child with the force of the current, and he would be gone again.

Dark, frightened eyes turned her way. Sunny grabbed for his flailing arm. She felt his shoulder dislocate as she and the current played a life-or-death tug-of-war with the child. But she maintained a steady pull, fighting the current that begged for both of them.

It seemed like an eternity until powerful hands behind her grasped the small child, pulled him from her grip, and handed him up a human chain of arms to safety.

Sunny faintly heard the cheers of the crowd before she slipped farther into the arroyo, struggling against the current. Suddenly jamming the toe of her running shoe against something unmovable, she felt excruciating pain ram up her leg. Fighting unconsciousness, she thought she heard someone call her name.

A gasp of pain kept her from swallowing water as she sank down into the dark current. Total blackness vanquished the terrorizing pain.

The soft whine of Prince Charming, his jaws clamped on to the shoulder of her life vest, nudged her back to reality. As arms lifted her to the edge of the current, her scream of pain pierced the air.

"My ankle!"

"Get a stretcher down here fast," one of the fire fighters yelled. "Let go of the rope. It's over. We've got the child."

"I can't," she sobbed. "My hand won't open."

As the blackness began to shade her body once more, she heard a faint voice. "I *know* this isn't according to procedure, but he goes with her to the hospital unless you want to try to separate his teeth from the vest. Remember, this dog's been trained to protect her at all costs. He hasn't let go of her since he got a hold of her in the water. Better hope he hangs on or he'll probably sink his teeth into one of us."

"Your room is already full of flowers and visitors—male, of course. Mike's nearly worn out the linoleum in there."

Sunny groaned in answer to the nurse's statement. It sounded as if the woman were shouting. She recognized the voice that came from the head of the gurney, but she couldn't quite put a face or name with it. She didn't care who was there. She wanted to stow away in the warm, dark world of the anesthesia once more—no light, no noise, no pain.

"Everybody out while we get her settled."

Crusty old bird, Sunny thought as she heard several people shuffling out of the room. Besides the fact that her eyelids were too heavy to lift, she didn't feel like seeing anyone.

Keeping her eyes closed, Sunny asked in a slightly slurred voice, "The child . . Are you sure he's okay?"

"He's a hell of a lot better off than you are. Did you have to try to save him single-handedly, Sunny?"

"Mike? What about Prince?" she asked as she slowly forced her eyes open.

"If I hadn't gotten to the hospital in time, he probably would have gone to surgery with you."

Sunny's eyes drifted shut, exhaustion and pain robbing her of coherent thought. She must have dozed off after they'd transferred her to the bed. At the sound of whispers, she forced her eyes open.

"Mike." Sunny searched his face. "What's the diagnosis?"

"Trimalleolar dislocation and fracture, Sunny. Dr. Johnson will be along to talk to you before too long. He had another emergency right after your surgery."

"Tell me what I want to know, Mike."

"Let's just say you're going to be laid up for a while."

"No way! I can work with a cast on, Mike."

The bustling, white-coated figure of the doctor appeared like a cyclone. "Wanting to get up and go to work already, Sunny? That even goes beyond your level of dedication. But it will be a little difficult, even for you—on crutches."

"Crutches?" she whispered. Her shoulders sank into the bed.

"This is a serious break, Sunny. It's broken in three places. I had to go in on both sides of your ankle and literally screw the broken pieces together. There's not a quick, six-week fix for this kind of break, but I'll talk to you more about that later. You need to rest now. I've ordered enough meds to keep you fairly comfortable."

As she closed her eyes, a lone tear slipped down her

cheek and ran into her ear. If she'd had the energy, she would have thrown her IV bag across the room.

The doctor's voice intruded. "Sunny, you're a hero in this city. You saved that child's life. He escaped with a few minor scrapes and bruises. Think of it this way. You deserve a vacation, compliments of the city."

Pinning the doctor with a lackluster gaze, she asked, "How long until my ankle is back to normal?" Sunny frowned as he glanced away before answering.

"Eight weeks in the cast. No weight on it at all because of the way we have it set. Don't mess up my work." The doctor paused to make sure she understood before continuing. "The rope burns on your hand and wrist will heal quickly. They'll be uncomfortable for a few days, but the scars will fade."

Sunny lifted her left hand and saw the gauze wrapping for the first time. The burning sensation was suddenly very real.

As the doctor started to leave, he added, "You're going to need some help for a while. Crutches will be impossible until your hand heals. I'll order a wheelchair for you."

Mike watched desperation cloud Sunny's eyes before she shut them. "The guys said the way you had the rope wrapped around your wrist and hand probably saved you from being swept away."

She must have fallen asleep. Her room was dark except for a light above the sink. Sunny squeezed her eyes tightly shut as memories of the day flooded her senses. She was thankful to be alive, but a dark feeling sat like a heavy weight on her chest, forcing despair into each crack and crevice of her heart.

With a groan, she tried to turn over onto her side. Feeling the heavy drag of the still damp cast, she rolled onto her back again. A broken ankle with an unwieldy cast was not in her plans. Her body felt weak. Her well-ordered life was floundering. With a flash, she recalled the last time her life had been in chaos.

She had been lying by the pool. The mower had suddenly zoomed across the lawn, but her dad had not been pushing it. When Sunny had glanced toward him, his face had been ashen with pain, his hands clawing at his chest. She'd been sixteen years old that day when she had dialed the hospital, begging for help.

Her mother had died five years before that. Since her father's heart attack, her focus had been clearly set. She had learned to depend on no one, absolutely no one, except herself. She was a survivor. If help was needed, she was the one to give, not the one to receive.

Now, at age thirty, she couldn't even get to the bathroom by herself. She couldn't even use the bedpan without someone's help. So much for independence.

"I'll be damned if I'll ask anyone for the bedpan," she yelled at the empty room. Her body jerked with angry sobs, her eyes flashed in pain. Grabbing the full glass of water that sat on the table next to the bed, she hurled it against the wall.

The old nightmare seized him with explosive force. His lungs were on fire, ready to explode. His strength and stamina exhausted, he could no longer fight the clawing current.

Drew bolted upright in bed. Nausea rolled like white water in his belly. The sheets tangled with his thrashing legs. Clammy, cold sweat covered his body. Spasms jerked the muscles in his leg. He gasped for air. A shudder convulsed his body with the fresh memory of icy water and the defying pain seconds after he had spotted the end of a log hurtling toward him.

A shiver shook his body as a drop of sweat trailed its way down his bare back. The deep, dark chill of the nightmare controlled him. Drew swiped at the sweat that ran into his eyes. The odor of fear hung in the air about him. It had been months since the last dream, yet the memories of that fateful day flashed like a neon sign in his mind. The news of Sunny's narrow escape had touched off his memories.

With trembling hands, Drew massaged the quadriceps above his left knee as he inhaled deep, shuddering breaths into his laboring lungs. Untangling the sheets from his legs, he eased off the bed and limped into the connecting bathroom.

Leaning over the Jacuzzi tub, he continued to massage his knee and dialed the arrow to hot on the faucet. As he sat down on the side of the tub, the cold porcelain against his bare skin barely penetrated the fog of his memories. Drew clenched his teeth and swallowed against the nausea. He stiffly swung his legs over the edge of the tub into the water, and with powerful shoulders, he maneuvered his body down into the steaming water.

He rested his head against the back of the oversize tub. The corded muscles in his neck stood out in relief, and his pulse continued to race. Drew banked his thundering thoughts as he stared out the window at the starless night. Gradually the heat of the pulsating water erased the spasms of pain and permeated the deep cold lodged within him. As his eyes drifted shut, he slipped deeper into the tub.

Sunny! The vision of swishing strawberry blond hair, upturned nose, and svelte figure danced across his eyelids. Mike's telephone call had shaken him, although at the time he'd told himself and Mike she was no concern of his. She wasn't—he didn't dare let her be. Yet he couldn't forget—she'd been there for him in the ER and during that long night after surgery.

He'd only seen her a few times, but the last weeks her image had been like a sassy little itch between his shoulder blades—he couldn't ignore it, but he didn't dare reach out to try to scratch the itch either. "Face it," he muttered to the dark room, "you may want to, but there's no escaping the thought of her."

He wondered how much Sunny's life would be affected by the accident. Would it cost her the career she loved? His cost had been high. The frown pinching his brow eased a bit. The reward had been great, too. Jesse. A smile lifted one corner of his mouth. He had pulled the rebellious drug addict out of the arroyo that day three years ago. He had become the homeless teenager's guardian, his family. He loved Jesse as though he were his own flesh and blood.

Drew refused to remember everything the arroyo had cost him. He *would* have to admit he'd never be the same person—no one would. He'd learned to keep the trauma he'd suffered in perspective, and he'd done fairly well, even during the times he'd seen Sunny recently. Until tonight, the bitter memory had begun to haze around the jagged edges. Now it felt as if fresh wounds were tearing at his soul.

Damn! His clenched fist hit the bubbling water, tossing droplets into the air, and waves over the edge of the tub.

As he pushed himself from the depths of the tub, water sluiced down his hair-roughened body, dripping onto the forest green carpet. He yanked a plush bath sheet from the shelf and briskly dried himself, as if, by hurrying, he could escape his thoughts. Tossing the towel over the side of the tub, he took a pair of black briefs from a drawer in the cabinet and stepped into them.

Opening the sliding glass door to the dawn of a new day, he stepped onto the frost-covered redwood deck. With concentrated effort, he pulled deep breaths of frigid air into his lungs, forcing the stubborn fragments of the nightmare from his mind.

Footprints, where the heavy frost melted under his

bare feet, followed him as he walked to the end of the deck that hung suspended from the side of the master suite. As he braced stiff arms against the railing, he looked at the snowcapped Sangre de Cristo Mountains, seeking the solace he so desperately wanted. Steam rose like a cloud around his damp body. He cocked his head; the sound of a powerful engine in the distance grew louder, ending the sanctuary he sought. Who the hell would be coming up the road to the ranch at this hour?

Tucking his flannel shirt into rumpled jeans, Drew heard the key turn in the lock as he stepped off the last stair. "What the hell are you doing here, Mike?"

Drew frowned at the grandfather clock as it struck the quarter hour. "Quarter to five. What's going on?" The muscles in his shoulders visibly tightened. "Is it Sunny?"

"Good morning to you, too," Mike drawled. Pleased with his brother's question, Mike smiled. "Is that coffee I smell?"

Confused, Drew shook his head. He didn't want to see anyone this morning. He wouldn't ask about her again; it had been a mistake in the first place. He walked toward the aroma of strong coffee, pushing open the swinging door of the kitchen.

"Look what the cat dragged in, Consuela," Drew said as he pulled out a chair and sat down at the round oak table, lifting his left leg up to rest it on the chair next to him.

Mike lifted the plump cook and swung her around. "Sure smells good in here. Got any waffle batter?"

"For you? Anytime. It'll just take me a minute."

Mike grabbed pottery mugs from the cupboard and poured two cups of the strong brew. "Mm, perfect. Have some, Drew. It might improve your disposition. I still can't believe you didn't realize who Sunny's father is. I'm positive I told you. I know there was talk that he was grooming you to fill his shoes as chief of police before you, um, left the department. You must have known him fairly well."

"Is there a point to this, Mike?"

"Sunny's going to need help until her hand heals, with her father away. She won't be able to use her crutches, and even then she shouldn't really be by herself. You know, it's difficult to manage on crutches."

The silence that followed lengthened to an unaccustomed awkwardness between the brothers. The only sound was the sizzle of the hot waffle iron. "I'd like her to recuperate here, but I thought I'd better check with you and Consuela first."

Drew jerked his leg off the chair beside him and sat up straight. "Good thing you checked. There's no way that would work out, no way in hell. Consuela has as much work as she can handle. Besides that, she's not a nurse, and this is not a convalescent home. There's no need to discuss it further."

He glared at Mike before turning toward the woman who had kept house for his family for the last twenty years. "Is breakfast almost ready, Consuela? I've got a lot of work to do."

Silence hung heavy over the breakfast table. The waffles were a toasty brown, and hot maple syrup with melted butter filled the little golden squares. Drew ate slowly, tasting nothing.

Consuela sat down at the table between the silent brothers. "It would be rather nice to have another woman in the house for a while. And she wouldn't be much work, I'm sure. Mike always tells me about what a special lady she is."

"Whose side are you on, anyway?" Drew blurted out as he tossed his wadded napkin onto the table. It landed on the plate.

Consuela frowned as she watched the napkin darken, absorbing the mixture of melted butter and syrup. "Side? Is this a competition or what?" She looked from

Drew's scowling face to Mike, who seemed to be engrossed in the sunrise framed in the bay window of the breakfast nook.

"The answer is no, Consuela. It's impossible."

Mike studied his brother. "You've always taken in strays."

Drew erupted from his chair and in a quiet but steely voice said, "Jesse and Rico are not strays! They are my family. They are *our* family. We are the only family either of them has, and don't ever forget it! And more to the point, Sunny is not a stray, nor could she ever be one. She's . . ." Drew's voice trailed off. He sat back down on the chair and rubbed the back of his neck.

"She's what?" Guessing at his brother's feeling, Mike pushed his advantage home. "Sunny has nowhere else to go. We've got that empty bedroom downstairs. It would be perfect. I have some say in this, Drew. Half of this ranch belongs to me, including the bedrooms. Would you turn a friend of mine away?"

"Just move her into your place. You two seem cozy enough."

Consuela gasped. "Drew, he can't do that! Your mama would never approve, and besides, Mike has to work. But if Sunny came here, it would be just fine. I vote yes."

"You don't have a vote. You're the cook."

Consuela took no offense. She could feel Drew erecting his defenses. She'd been here after his accident. She understood. "I most certainly do have a vote in this. I do the work around here, and I was the excuse you used. You're not going to hide behind my skirts. Maybe we would have listened if you'd given the real reason."

Mike smiled broadly as he stood up and stretched. "That's two to one; it's settled then. I've got to shove off. My shift starts in just a little over an hour. I'll call you tonight and let you know when Sunny will be released from the hospital.''

For the rest of the day, Drew debated with himself. There was no way he would allow that woman in his home. She had already invaded the privacy of his mind. He'd drive into Albuquerque and straighten out this mess. He'd help make arrangements for her recuperation, but he couldn't allow her further invasion into his life.

Sunny sat up straight in the hospital bed and looked at Mike. ''I can't believe you cooked this up without consulting me.'' Taking a deep breath, she continued, ''There's not a reason in the world why I shouldn't stay at home. I'll sleep downstairs on the sofa until I can get around on my crutches.''

Sunny glanced at the crutches that leaned against the wall, then at the wheelchair that sat next to the bed. Each time she lowered her leg to the floor, her toes turned blue and the pounding pain was too much to endure.

She turned pleading eyes toward Mike. ''You know this won't work, Mike. He's your brother and you love him, but you've seen how uncomfortable we are around each other. Besides that, the man is a boar.'' Sunny leaned back and closed her eyes.

Mike chuckled. ''Yes, I think you've mentioned—''

The sudden silence was deafening. Sunny slowly turned her head. Drew. An antique brown leather bomber jacket covered his broad shoulders. Her gaze drifted lower—anywhere but his face. He was perfectly turned out in dark brown slacks with a cream-colored shirt tucked into them, and soft leather loafers.

She glanced up. How much of this conversation had he heard? Judging by his expression, he'd been listening far too long. She could see his eyes had turned almost black. His look pinned her against the hospital bed.

It felt as if the thermostat were stuck on sixty degrees. She needed to pull the covers up to her chin. She hadn't thought a thing about lying here in her cotton nightgown—until now. Suddenly she felt naked and vulnerable. If only she could reach her robe or the sheet. Sunny tucked her right foot under her; at least her bare leg wasn't exposed anymore.

Drew nodded to his brother before his glance drifted toward Sunny again. "Can I talk to you, Mike? Out in the hall."

A minute later, Mike stuck his head in the door and said, "I'll call you later, Sun."

Before she could object, Mike disappeared down the hall, and Drew stepped into the room. Sunny studied him as he walked to the window. Keeping his back to her, he stared out the window. She glanced away when he turned toward her, but instead of saying anything, he leaned against the windowsill, his long legs crossed at the ankles.

He rubbed the back of his neck and closed his eyes before looking at her again. Sunny looked virginal. Drew snorted. The very thought was absurd. The white gown covered her well enough. It looked almost prim, but soft, alluring. His gaze rested on the translucence of her skin. Light blue veins mapped their path across her chest, disappearing below the scoop neckline. Tiny buttons began just above her breasts and were hooked through little loops. It would take a man a night and a half to undo them. His eyes followed the descending line. The gown appeared a little darker where her nipples puckered against the fabric.

A muscle jumped in the side of his jaw as his eyes focused on each button until he saw the last one a few inches below her waist. The gown ended just below her knees where the cast started on her left leg. Her right leg must be tucked under her bottom. He could only see part of her bent knee where a dimple seemed to wink at him.

He glanced at the cast. It was a blinding white until it reached the ankle. Blood had oozed through the heavy cast on both sides—fresh, crimson red. Her toes looked like puffy little purple clouds.

Drew realized he'd been staring. He felt cold and hot simultaneously. Memories of his own hospitalization swept over him. He hated hospitals and he hated seeing Sunny here.

"Drew?" Sunny's soft voice slipped through the fog that seemed to hover around him. "I'm sorry about what you overheard."

"It doesn't matter." He stood and shrugged his shoulders. "Mike and I have arranged for you to stay at the ranch."

"I don't think that's a good idea."

Drew looked at her, rubbing the tight muscles in his neck. "You were there for me once." He cleared his throat. "I'm simply returning the favor."

"I didn't come to your room as a favor. It was more than that." When Drew turned his back on her words, she stopped talking. He was the one who had refused to see her again. She wanted to ask him why, but she wouldn't.

Sunny folded her arms under her breasts and took a deep breath. "I guess I don't have much choice, but I'll have to bring my dog with me."

Drew stared. She sounded like a defiant child. She looked all woman. He stared at the soft flesh she'd exposed with her position and said, "Mike explained to me about the dog. I'll stay at Mike's tonight. Be ready by about ten. I'll pick up the dog and pack your things in the morning."

"Oh, God. No." Sunny muttered even as her face flamed. This man was *not* going to handle her clothing.

Thoughts of the elegant new lingerie that lay between folds of tissue in the boxes on her bed deepened her blush. She refused to imagine the delicate silk and satin in his callused hands.

"How can I be ready? I don't have anything here to wear."

Drew turned back toward Sunny and flicked what he hoped was a casual glance her way. "I've worn a cast before. You'll only be able to get certain things on over it. I'll bring something for you to wear when I pick you up. Good night."

Sunny awakened at dawn. A combination of anxiety and anticipation prevented her from drifting back to sleep. Her body felt stiff and sore, but the pain in her ankle had subsided to an almost tolerable throb. A sponge bath and shampoo sapped her energy. Eight weeks until the cast came off—an eternity.

She sat quietly in a chair, belted snugly in her chenille robe, her arms anchored tightly around her body. Her leg was propped up on another chair. She'd called her father and reassured him she would be fine.

She worried her bottom lip with her teeth. Dr. Johnson had stopped by earlier. He'd changed the bandage on her hand and signed her discharge papers. She closed her eyes against the words that continued to echo in her mind. With this type of fracture, there was a chance she wouldn't be able to jog mile after mile as she'd done in the past. Only time would tell.

Her mind flashed to Drew, remembering his grit in the emergency room, recalling the bitterness in his words the day he'd been broadsided. Understanding a small portion of what he must have felt, she closed her eyes.

She didn't want to go anywhere with Drew, and especially not to his home. She wanted to get on with her plans—her life. She'd never been around anyone before who made her feel the way he did—uncomfortable, angry, even tongue-tied.

She wouldn't impose on him any longer than necessary. She'd come back to Albuquerque as soon as possible. Sunny sighed in defeat and opened her eyes. He stood, framed in the doorway, one hip cocked in an arrogant stance.

She smiled tentatively, but he regarded her with what felt like a critical eye. In one hand, he held a piece of her luggage. Walking over to the bed, he unzipped the bag and pulled out her turquoise sweat suit, laying it neatly on the bed.

"We'll have to cut the seam up the leg."

Sunny caught her breath as he slowly pulled her new aqua chemise and matching French-cut panties out of the bag. She watched as he dangled the chemise by the spaghetti straps over one hand and caressed the silk of the panties with his fingers.

Drew looked at Sunny. "By the looks of the contents in those boxes on your bed, I'd say you were plotting the seduction of some unsuspecting man. An affair while Daddy's away, Sunny? Who did you have in mind? My brother?"

Sunny blanched under his quiet but lethal attack. Her anger was immediate and acidic. "Who?" She smiled sweetly. "Why you, of course." Sunny watched color flush up his neck and flood his face. A pulse hammered in his throat.

Drew stared at her. She couldn't be serious. His hands clenched into fists before he dropped the delicacies as if he'd been burnt. The sight of the intimate apparel in the boxes had really gotten to him. Just the thought of the silk caressing her body had brought a sweat to his forehead. "I'll send someone in to help you dress. Hurry. Your Prince Charming doesn't seem too patient," he said as the door swung shut behind him.

FOUR

"Damn, what are those vultures doing here?" He should have considered this possibility. Reporters were always out for a story. They should have left through a back entrance.

Sunny glanced up at Drew, wondering what he was talking about, but before she could ask, she heard the sharp bark of Prince Charming's welcome. She smiled as she spotted him with his head hung out of the open window of a midnight blue Thunderbird.

As Drew opened the door, Prince bounded out of the car and slid to a stop beside Sunny. His body trembled with barely contained excitement. With his front feet on the arm of the wheelchair, he greeted his mistress with sloppy exuberance. Sunny tightly hugged his neck and buried her face in his thick coat before drawing back to speak to the dog in a low, melodious voice.

The nurse stood patiently behind the wheelchair. Television cameras rolled, capturing the touching reunion of the dog and the city's latest hero.

Sunny glanced up, surprised to see several reporters and cameramen a few feet away. Why were they here?

She looked for Drew, but he was busy stowing her belongings in the backseat of the car.

Drew watched as Sunny answered the questions each reporter asked, deflecting the praise that was offered her, turning her actions into a matter of duty, stating anyone would have done the same. Her dog sat next to her, alert, ready to protect her at a moment's notice. After a few minutes, Drew could see her tiring. He debated with himself whether he should step in and help, or stay in the background to avoid calling attention to himself. But before he could make a choice, she glanced at him.

"Thanks for your concern and interest, everyone, but I see my ride is here," she said politely.

A smile tugged at the corner of his mouth. He'd never been described quite that way before. The cameras suddenly swung his way, and microphones were stuck in his face. Questions, which he ignored, hit him like pellets as he commanded the dog to get in the backseat and helped Sunny into the car. Without a word to Sunny or the reporters who continued to pursue him, Drew crouched beside the open car door. He pulled two large pillows from the back and gently eased them under and around her cast. He checked her seat belt and closed the door. Folding the wheelchair, he placed it in the trunk.

"I know who you are," one of the reporters shouted.

Drew glared at the ambitious reporter as he shut the trunk with unnecessary force, but the man didn't flinch under Drew's glare.

"Drew Williams," he shouted. "*Lieutenant* Drew Williams."

Recognition filtered through the group of reporters, and with a new fervor, questions began again.

"What's your relationship to Ms. Steele?"

Ignoring the reporters, Drew slid into the driver's seat. Releasing a breath he hadn't realized he'd been hoarding, he looked at the pale woman in the seat next to him.

"Thank goodness they can't see through these tinted windows. Are you comfortable?"

"I'm okay," Sunny murmured as she rested her head against the back of the seat and closed her eyes. She wanted to tell him to go to hell, that she was going home—her own home. But instead she said, "I've never been so tired in my life, and I hate imposing on you. I don't want to go."

Somehow Sunny knew she would never be able to backtrack to where her life had been just a few days ago. Life, as she had always known it, had been permanently detoured.

She felt Drew's gaze flick over her as they continued to sit in the car in front of the hospital. Why didn't he just drive and get this over with? What was he waiting for? Some sign from her that she wanted to go? Hardly.

With a soft whine, Prince wedged his head between the bucket seats. Sunny turned her head and reached up with her bandaged hand, rubbing the dog's neck. "His Dramamine!" Her eyes went to the man beside her. His eyes seemed to soften for a moment. Since they had walked out of the hospital, Drew's attitude had in some way altered. He changed like a chameleon, and she was beginning to learn he did the unexpected. "Mike told me about it. I looked around until I found it. I can't believe he really gets carsick. Are you sure he won't throw up all over my car?"

Sunny smiled at the thought. "He won't. He'll probably sleep most of the way. The medication makes him drowsy."

Their eyes met and held. Sunny felt compelled to go on. "I really am sorry about intruding in your life. I'll stay out of your way as much as I can."

Drew realized she was serious, and nodded. He started the engine, slipped on his sunglasses, and pulled away from the curb before he spoke. "I won't be there too much anyway. I've got a couple of trips I have to make in the next few weeks."

"Trips?"

"I work for the governor. I'm available to communities throughout the state to train law enforcement personnel in methods of dealing with drug runners and how to infiltrate their organizations."

"Oh, I had no idea."

"I only took the position after the governor agreed to let me keep a very low profile—no television, no announcing what I was doing or where I was going." When he noticed Sunny's frown, he added, "We don't want it to be public knowledge for obvious reasons. There have been a few threats made against me over the years. So we simply don't advertise the where and what of my job."

"Threats?"

"It's not that uncommon."

"I know. My dad's had his share, though he always tried to downplay them."

Sunny concentrated on the purr of the engine and the soft click of the turn signal as Drew moved through traffic, picking up speed as the car merged onto the northbound freeway. The pain in her ankle began to gnaw at her, but she refused to let the tears, which seemed just a swallow and a blink away these days, fall. She understood tears were a normal reaction to the trauma and surgery she'd undergone, but they made her feel at an even greater disadvantage.

Her body gradually relaxed, yet her senses were fine-tuned to a keen awareness of the man next to her. His male scent mingled with the antiseptic smell that clung to her from the days she'd spent in the hospital. After a few miles, the motion of the car lulled Sunny into a light sleep.

Looking over at Sunny, and then at the dog whose

head rested close to his mistress's, Drew noticed that both of them were asleep. He reached over and lightly touched Sunny's hair with the back of his hand. Silk. Prince opened his eyes and nuzzled closer to his mistress. Drew surprised himself with the words he uttered quietly to the dog. "Don't worry, boy, I won't hurt her."

Drew took a deep breath. If anyone got hurt . . . Could she really be planning to seduce him? He was afraid it wouldn't take much effort on her part. If she weren't the marrying type . . . He had no intention of ever marrying.

Until she'd said he was her choice, she'd seemed unaware of him as a man—matter of fact, she still did. He'd never met anyone like her. She seemed oblivious to her own beauty, to her own sensuality. She was a madcap mixture—a concoction of soft, feminine fragility and a tough, enduring strength. It had taken a compassionate but gutsy lady to step into that arroyo, placing her own life on the line to rescue the life of a child. It was a compelling combination with which he had no wish to tangle.

And those boxes and bags of new clothing on her bed. He'd opened each one of them. Once he'd looked in the first one, there was no restraint strong enough to keep him from reaching into every one and pulling out the items for further examination. She'd obviously purchased them shortly before her accident, because she hadn't even put them away. He now knew her sizes and her tastes. Her sizes indicated a lusciousness she didn't readily reveal, and her tastes ran to the expensive and ultrafeminine—satin and silk and lace. No imitations for Sunny. She would be a handful in more ways than one.

A soft moan from his passenger brought a halt to his wandering imagination. Uncomfortable, Drew took another deep breath, squirmed in the confining seat belt, and adjusted his jeans in an attempt to make the fit more comfortable.

The nagging pain increased, dragging Sunny back to the present. The car was no longer silent. Music, soft though it was, poured from the powerful stereo. It took her a moment to recognize the sweet, sensuous wails of Kenny G's saxophone. She had the same compact disc in her collection at home. Home. If only that were where she was going now.

A lone tear pooled and slid down Sunny's pale cheek. She didn't understand all the feelings rioting inside of her. Her ankle felt as though someone had branded it with a red-hot iron. She should have given in and taken a pain pill before she'd left the hospital. If the pain were lessened, things might not look quite so bleak.

As if Prince understood her pain, he let out a long, soft whine and wedged his head farther between the bucket seats. Sunny reached up with her gauze-en-wrapped hand to touch his neck. He lapped the solitary tear as she turned toward him, her head resting on the high back of the seat. His gentle ministration coaxed another tear to form and slip down her cheek.

Sunny's life had crumbled at her feet. For the first time in years, she didn't have options or choices. This man beside her was a stranger—nothing like the man she'd thought she'd encountered three years ago. Had she romanticized what she'd felt? His current behavior proved he had feet of clay. Her tears were coming faster, and there was not a thing she could do to stop them.

Drew glanced over at Sunny as the dog licked her face. He was certain she'd been asleep. Tears streaked down her face, slowly yet persistently. She didn't sob. She didn't make a sound. She didn't move. Prince whined again.

Sunny's face appeared to lose more color even as he

momentarily took his gaze off the road to glance at her again. He scowled at the highway. Maybe she should have stayed in the hospital another day or two. No, he knew that wasn't the answer. He didn't want to deal with the understanding, the empathy, he felt for her. He knew what was happening all too well. He didn't want to, but he did. He would bet that her tears were not only for the pain but for the confusion she felt. He'd shed more than a few tears himself in those early days. Could he give her the support she would need yet not risk his own emotional stability, for which he'd fought so hard?

"Sunny?" he asked as he reached over and covered her injured hand. "Everything is going to be okay. The pain will gradually lessen—honest. You'll soon be back on your feet. You're going to come through this fine." He hesitated. "How soon can you have another pain pill?" he asked as he drove the Thunderbird onto the shoulder at the edge of the freeway and turned off the engine. Flicking on the hazard lights, Drew removed his sunglasses and looked directly at her.

The tears slowed a bit, but she still didn't respond. Drew unbuckled his seat belt, lowered the volume on the stereo, and turned toward her. Reaching down, he lifted her cast and adjusted one of the pillows. "Talk to me, Sunny. When did you last take a pill?"

Sunny swiped at her tears before answering, "Last night."

"Last night?" Drew echoed in disbelief. "I know they gave you a prescription for pain. Where are they, and why aren't you taking them?" Pushing the dog aside, Drew reached for her purse on the backseat and opened it.

"Don't paw through my things. I don't want a pill," she answered as she brushed at her tears again. Sunny took the tissues he offered and blew her nose before adding, "They make me feel woozy."

"That won't matter in the least since you're not the one driving. You can sleep the rest of the way home. You're white as a sheet, and we still have thirty miles to go." He dug through her bag looking for the container that had evidently settled to the bottom of her oversize bag.

"Why on earth do you carry all this stuff around with you? There's everything imaginable in here and then some."

"Drew, I'm beginning to feel really angry with you."

He glanced up at her before going back to his dig. "Good. At least you have a little color in your cheeks now." He found the brown plastic container, read the directions, and shook out two capsules.

He pulled a thermos from the backseat. "Consuela sent coffee. Decaf. She's on a health kick this week." Unscrewing the metal cup, he poured the coffee, then sipped it.

Fascinated, Sunny watched his top lip curl over the cup and taste the coffee.

He placed the capsules in her uninjured hand. "The coffee isn't too hot."

Sunny looked up at him. Their eyes met, dueled. She accepted the inevitable. Once again she was in a no-win situation with Drew, but she didn't have the energy to argue. And at this point, she didn't think arguing was what she wanted to do anyway. Without taking her eyes away from his, she swallowed the pills. Once again an unspoken truce settled between them.

For the first time since she'd stepped into the cold current of the arroyo, Sunny felt safe. She didn't understand why, but she instinctively knew that she had nothing to fear from this man. Drew would never intentionally hurt her.

Taking the empty cup from her, he refilled it and

drank a few swallows of coffee before handing it back to Sunny.

"Drew, I didn't mean what I said."

He glanced at her and then quickly away. He fidgeted with sunglasses that were on the dash. He frowned. He was waiting for the medication to take effect before he drove on. And in the meantime, he didn't care to get into anything personal. His curiosity finally won out. "Which time are you talking about? You've said several things I can think of that you might want to apologize for."

Color stained her cheeks. "I'm not apologizing."

His frown deepened further as he waited for her to go on. She didn't. He turned off the tape. "So you meant everything you've said?" His frown disappeared as he looked toward her again and raised his eyebrows in question.

"I'm not saying that." The air crackled with an odd sort of tension. How could he be so kind one moment and an arrogant cynic the next? "Please, let me say this." Her hands trembled. The coffee sloshed onto the bandage that covered her hand. She watched the brown stain spread and seep into the gauze.

"Go for it." A grin lifted one side of his mouth, but his eyes remained wary.

"What I said at the hospital this morning about . . ." She took another sip of coffee.

"Seducing me?"

Sunny spluttered and choked. She glanced at him. He was toying with her. She studied the coffee and plunged ahead.

"I didn't mean it. I reacted to your taunt. Even if I wanted to, I wouldn't know how."

He threw back his head and laughed. Between his dying chuckles he gasped, "That's the funniest thing I've ever heard. Do you enjoy playing the part of the innocent virgin?"

Before she could stop herself, the words rushed out. "It's not a part I'm playing. It's the god-awful truth. Satisfied?"

Prince gave a sharp bark.

His heart jerked in his chest. "Hardly," Drew muttered under his breath. There was nothing amusing about *this*. He pulled his sunglasses off the dashboard and jammed them onto his face. She thought she didn't know how to seduce a man! She'd seduced him more times than he could count in his dreams. His body went out of control every time he came near her.

What had he gotten himself into? A thirty-year-old virgin was an anachronism in this day and age. He could barely fathom such an oddity, but she'd said it; rather, she'd yelled it with conviction.

He knew it was the *god-awful* truth—not the pain medication loosening her tongue. The knowledge sent a surge of unwanted emotions through his body—feelings with which he was unfamiliar, feelings that scared the hell out of him.

Drew took the cup from her. Wishing it were whiskey, he gulped the last of the coffee. He returned the thermos to the backseat, fastened his seat belt, started the engine, and pulled back into the traffic.

When he glanced at Sunny a few moments later, she was sleeping. Sleeping as if their conversation had never happened. Sleeping the sleep of innocence. He knew it was due to the medication he'd forced her to take. Nevertheless, he resented it. He felt spent, ancient, jaded.

He pulled to a stop in front of his house. He had the feeling that once Sunny entered his home, nothing and no one would ever be the same. Resentment filled his eyes as he turned toward her. "Sunny, we're here." His voice did not stir her. "Sunny!" He reached over, his hand hesitant, before he touched her arm. Drew watched as she awakened slowly.

Eyes heavy, Sunny glanced at him and then looked at the two-story brick home. "You have a beautiful home, Drew."

Drew slipped out of the car and went to the trunk. Realization hit him. Her wheelchair wouldn't maneuver in the soft gravel. Slamming the lid of the trunk, he went to the passenger side and opened the door. He reached down and removed the pillows. "I'll carry you. The chair won't move through the soft gravel."

Sunny glanced at his closed face as he lifted her.

Her scent. The heat of her body felt like an inferno. Her legs dangled across his arms. He could feel the fullness of her breasts as she curled against him. She probably weighed one fifteen—just as Mike thought. Mike. The picture of them hugging flashed through his mind. Drew tried to keep the image focused—it faded.

She was soft and warm. Her hair blew across his mouth, feeling silky soft, its scent seducing him. Drew wanted to quicken his pace, but his knee wouldn't allow it. He walked down the hall to the bedroom, sat her on the bed, and stepped back. In a husky voice he said, "I'll get your bags from the car."

Sunny glanced around the room. She sat on a chaise lounge that was upholstered in a nubby peach-colored fabric and looked at her surroundings. It wasn't a simple bedroom. It was a suite with a roomy sitting area and a bathroom large enough to accommodate the wheelchair. The entire area was decorated in peach and cream. Chintz, plaid, solid, and striped fabrics harmonized to give a restful atmosphere to the large room. On the east wall there was a bay window with upholstered cushions on the seat underneath it. The Sangre de Cristo Mountains seemed only an arm's length away. A small antique desk sat in one corner, and an entertainment center with a television and small stereo system was placed so it could be enjoyed from either the sitting area or the bed.

Consuela had brought her dinner on a bed tray a few minutes ago. The thick beef stew and crusty French bread were a welcome change from hospital food. Prince sprawled beside her on the polished oak floor.

While the housekeeper had helped her settle in this afternoon, she had explained to Sunny that the suite had been remodeled and decorated for Mrs. Williams, Drew and Mike's mother. After her husband's death, she'd no longer wanted to stay in the master suite upstairs. A few months ago, she'd grown tired of the isolation of the ranch, and though she enjoyed good health, she now lived in a retirement complex in Santa Fe where many of her friends resided. The housekeeper had also mentioned that Drew had personally checked over the room this morning. He had rolled up the area rugs and stored them.

After the bustle and noise of the hospital, Sunny was enjoying the serenity of the room. She had not seen Drew since he'd delivered her things. Rico had shyly said hi from the doorway. She needed to speak to Drew about him. She would need his permission to see if Rico could feed and exercise Prince.

The quiet was broken with Drew's shout. "Rico, don't go in there."

Prince jumped to his feet as the young boy came bounding through the doorway. "Sunny! Sunny, you're on TV. Dad, too," he shouted over his shoulder as he grabbed the remote from the table beside the lounge and tuned the set to the local news.

"Our human interest feature for this week is about people we've seen in the news before. Sunny Steele, the daughter of our former police chief, Joe Steele, was released from the hospital this morning. As you recall, Ms. Steele risked her life last week to save a young boy who was caught in the flooding Embudo Arroyo. She was hospitalized, and underwent surgery for a fractured ankle. She answered a few questions for our reporter."

Sunny listened as they showed the impromptu interview outside the hospital. As it ended, pictures of the arroyo rescue flashed on the screen before the anchor team continued the story.

"Retired Police Lieutenant Drew Williams was at the hospital to pick up Ms. Steele. The lieutenant suffered a similar accident three years ago when he also heroically saved the life of a teenager. Lieutenant Williams requested and received the guardianship of the fifteen-year-old, who was a drug addict and homeless at the time of the arroyo incident. We have learned that the young man has successfully been through treatment and is now studying at the University of New Mexico.

"Ms. Steele's dog, whose name we understand is Prince Charming, also accompanied Drew Williams. Their destination upon leaving the hospital is unknown.

"As you may remember, Lieutenant Williams is well known for the major role he played in several major drug busts in this area before his early retirement. The last and biggest bust shortly before his retirement was the Granger case. Gus Granger is currently serving a life sentence for first-degree murder in the state penitentiary, largely due to the lieutenant's infiltration into the biggest drug ring in the state's history.

"Another interesting sidelight to this story is that Drew Williams' brother, Mike Williams, is Ms. Steele's partner. They both work as paramedics for the city.

"Detective Williams refused to answer any questions outside the hospital this morning."

Sunny's spoon hovered in the air between her gaping mouth and the steaming bowl of stew as she watched the anchor team of the news station report the story.

"Wow! Neat-o! Maybe you're on another station, too," Rico said as he began to run through the channels.

"I've seen enough, Rico. Please, wash up for dinner."

Sunny's spoon clattered against the pottery bowl as she turned toward the door, where Drew stood stiffly, staring at the blackening TV screen.

"I can't believe they put all that on television," Sunny began. "Don't they have anything better to report? Like a bank robbery or a murder?"

Drew stared at the blank screen and muttered an unrepeatable oath before he turned on his heel and shut the door quietly with an ominous click.

No longer hungry, Sunny placed the tray of food on the table beside her. She'd learned more about Drew in the last five minutes than she could assimilate. She'd known about his accident, but other than that, it was all news to her.

Standing at the bathroom sink the next morning, Sunny balanced on one foot while she attempted a quick wash and brushed her hair. Dark circles shadowed her eyes. She plopped back into the wheelchair, exhausted.

She still puzzled over who had come into her bedroom last night. She knew the door was closed when she'd fallen asleep, but when she'd awakened early this morning, it was ajar.

A soft knock sounded on the bedroom door, and Consuela came through with a tray. "Good morning. I brought the morning paper. I rescued it just as Drew started to throw it in the fireplace. Front-page story, pictures, the works." Consuela placed the tray on Sunny's lap and opened the newspaper.

"I'll read it later. Breakfast looks delicious."

"Okay then, I'll get on with my chores. Ring the bell if you need anything." She tugged at the apron that covered her ample form before adding, "You look a little peaked this morning. Eat up. You'll feel a lot better."

Sunny opened the newspaper and studied the picture. She heard the muted ring of the phone as she began to eat.

Drew knocked once and entered, a portable phone in one hand and gauze dressings in the other. He gave her the phone. "Mike wants to speak to you. Don't be too long. I want to bandage your hand."

Sunny waited for Drew to leave the room before she spoke to Mike, but he sat down in the overstuffed chair opposite her instead. Looking at the mountains out the window, she attempted to blank from her mind the man who sat so close, she could smell the clean male scent of him.

"Mike?"

"Hi, Sun. You're a front-page celebrity. Congratulations. As I told Drew, that picture spoke more than a thousand words. Quite the cozy couple. Fast work, Sunny. You and Drew were the human interest story last night on the six-o'clock news, too." Mike paused, but when Sunny didn't respond, he went on, "My brother doesn't sound too happy about any of it."

"I know."

"Why do I get the feeling you can't say much right now?"

"I'd better go. He wants to bandage my hand." She looked straight at Drew, who hadn't taken his eyes off her as she spoke with his brother. "I need to explain I can take care of it myself."

Reaching over, Drew took the phone from Sunny. "Mike, Sunny's busy right now. I'll be talking to you soon. 'Bye."

Sunny could hear Mike continuing to talk before Drew pushed the off button, breaking the connection. "Wasn't that rather rude?" She reached over and touched the power switch on the remote. Keeping her eyes on the *Today Show*, she began eating.

"When you're finished pushing your food around on your plate, I'll bandage your hand."

"I'd rather do it myself, thank you," she answered, setting the breakfast tray on the floor beside her.

"So you said." Drew watched the German shepherd lift his head and look at the food that remained on the plate. "Won't that dog eat the rest?"

"No," she answered absently. "Oh, no. I forgot. Did someone try to feed him last night?"

"I put food out for him, but he hasn't touched it."

"Poor Prince. He must be starved. He won't eat a bite unless he's given a release word which means it's okay for him to start. It prevents a dog from ever being poisoned. Would you please take him out to his bowl and say, 'apple'?"

"Seriously?"

"Yes. Please?"

Drew returned a few minutes later. "He's really well trained. Mike told me how you got him."

"Would it be okay if Rico took over his feeding each evening and exercised him for me? He's used to jogging several miles a week with me. But I don't want anyone except you and Rico to know his release word, okay?"

"Sure, but there's no one around this ranch who would harm a dog. Most of my men have been here for years. We only have one fairly new hand, and I thoroughly checked him out."

"I'm sure that's true, but I want to keep him within the bounds of his training, with only one person responsible for his care."

"All right. I'll have Rico come by and see you about it after school."

Drew sat down across from her again. "Now, let me see your hand." When she clutched her hand to her chest in refusal, he went on in a soothing tone as if talking to a belligerent child. "The nurse gave me instructions yesterday, Sunny."

The housekeeper came in, made Sunny's bed, and picked up the tray, chattering the entire time. By the time she left, Sunny realized Drew had taken her hand and was cutting off the bandage. She watched as his large, callused hands unwrapped the gauze.

His breath hissed out. "You really had a grip on that rope, didn't you?" He glanced up, and their eyes met in understanding. A shudder shook him as he pictured her in the rushing water. He wanted to bring her palm to his lips—instead he muttered, "Good thing or you probably wouldn't be here."

He applied the antibiotic ointment to the burns. His gentleness surprised her. He appeared so tough and uncaring at times. But she was beginning to realize it was a facade.

Something else surprised her—her awareness of him as a man. She had seen hundreds of men—naked men—in her career. She had bathed them and taken care of them, but none of them had affected her as Drew, who sat here fully clothed, was beginning to. Sunny frowned. An unfamiliar rush of feeling raced up her arm as his thumb slid across her wrist.

"There now, that wasn't so bad, was it?"

"No, not at all. Thank you."

"You look flushed. You're not running a fever, are you?"

Her hands flew to her hot cheeks. "No. I'm sure. It must be my hand. It's a little painful."

Drew didn't believe her for a moment, but he'd let it go for now. She seemed flustered. He'd check on her later to make certain there wasn't some kind of infection setting in. He picked up the supplies and started toward the door.

"Did you read the morning paper?" Sunny blurted.

Drew turned back toward her. She wasn't acting like her usual, calm self. "Yes. Did you?"

"No, I saw the picture. That was enough. Maybe I'll read it later. I'm sorry you were dragged into all of this. I had no idea this state was so hard up for news." Sunny watched as he shrugged his shoulders.

The following days became a routine of sorts. Consuela popped in and out of her room, bringing meals, fresh laundry, a variety of books and magazines, and an endless store of gossip and idle chatter. Sunny had asked her a couple of questions about Drew, but after a long, speculative look from the housekeeper, Sunny had decided not to ask anything else.

She and Rico became friends. He blitzed in and out, with Prince hot on his heels. He'd cheerfully taken over the care of the dog. She taught Rico how to work with Prince, how to whistle for him, and the commands to use to make him obey.

This morning, as it was every morning, her door had been opened after she'd gone to sleep. She sighed as she looked in the bathroom mirror, brushing her hair. He had been in her dreams again last night. She'd decided it had to be Drew who checked on her with such consistency. The thought of him looking at her while she slept was unsettling.

He came in each morning after breakfast to bandage her hand. A guarded respect had gradually developed between them. She continued to try to piece together the many different aspects of him she was beginning to discover. Moody and restless, Sunny longed to be out of doors. She hadn't left the suite of rooms, lovely though it was, and she needed a change.

When Sunny wheeled the chair out of the bathroom a few minutes later, he was there. His hands were shoved into the back pockets of his worn jeans, pulling them tight—tighter than usual. As Drew turned from the bay window, she quickly raised her stare to his face.

Watching her, Drew removed his hands from the pockets and commented, "I wondered how you made that thing move with one working hand and one foot."

"Quite a sight, aren't I?"

"That's for sure." He wasn't speaking about the jerky way she maneuvered the chair across the room. He was looking at the woman. She wore a nightshirt on which Garfield was sprawled in leisurely fashion yawning some absurdity that he couldn't quite read without staring. Was it possible to be jealous of a fictitious cat?

"Drew?" She wanted to squirm under his gaze, to tug at the nightshirt, which had scooted up to the middle of her thighs.

Their eyes met. Abruptly Drew turned toward the door, calling over his shoulder, "Get dressed, Sunny. I'll be back in a little while. I want to talk to you."

He wanted to talk? He seldom said more than a few sentences. She quickly wriggled herself into another jogging suit, regretting how limited her wardrobe was these days.

When Drew returned a few minutes later, he closed the door. Every other time he'd come into her room, he'd made certain the door was left open. Sunny turned off the TV.

Drew went into the bathroom and got the gauze and tape. He didn't say a word as he unwrapped the bandages and studied her palm. "I think it's healed enough to leave off the dressing."

"I agree." Sunny opened and closed her fingers a few times. "It feels better without the bandage. Thanks." She pushed her chair away from him, away from the male scent of him, away from the temptation to reach out and touch him.

"I called Mike. He and Jesse, my son, are driving up tonight. They'll be staying for the weekend. I'm sure you'll be happy to see Mike. They'll be here in time for a late dinner. Would you like to eat with the family tonight?"

"I'd love to. I need a change."

"I imagine cabin fever's about to take over, right?"

"How'd you know?"

"I've been there, remember? Which is what I wanted to talk to you about." He paced to the window and came back to the chair and sat down. "Did Mike ever tell you about Jesse?"

She shook her head. "Not really. He told me you had two boys, but he didn't say much more."

Drew nodded. "I want you to know my version of some of this, not the romanticized media tale." He shook his head in disgust.

"As you already know, I saved Jesse's life three years ago. It was like your situation. I was at the right place at the right time, or the wrong place at the wrong time, however you want to look at it. Jesse was almost sixteen at the time. He'd been skateboarding in the arroyo." Drew hesitated, hating the images that flashed through his mind. He took a deep breath.

"He came to see me in the hospital, to thank me for saving his life. I knew by then that my career was over. Dr. Johnson made certain I understood that fact." Seeing Sunny's frown, he hurried on, "Your dad offered me a desk job. I didn't want it. If I couldn't be out in the field doing what I loved, I didn't want any of it. Maybe if I'd been a few years older . . . I don't know. It took me a while to accept it. I chose an early retirement."

Leaning his forearms on his thighs and clasping his hands, Drew stared at the floor. "Jesse came to see me several times while I was in the hospital. He opened up to me. I found out he had no home—nothing except the clothes on his back and the skateboard he'd lost in the arroyo. And if the truth were known, it was probably stolen.''

Drew shook his head. He hated remembering. ''In order to eat, he stole any food he could find. He'd lived in abandoned buildings or wherever he could crash for the night. The year before, he had come home one day, and his mother and her boyfriend had left without a word. The super in their building had changed the locks on the apartment. Jesse had no place to go, and his mother had taken everything.

''He was an angry, hurting boy with world-weary eyes. He was also a hard-core drug addict. I think almost drowning got his attention. I believe he was subconsciously asking me for help by telling me about all of this. Little bits and pieces of it came out during that week I was in the hospital. A couple of times when he came to see me, he was stoned and probably revealed more than he realized.''

Drew leaned back in the chair again and looked at Sunny. Making a decision, he admitted, ''I was angry, too. Somehow we each had something the other one needed. To make a long and involved story short, he agreed to go into treatment for his addiction, and I applied for guardianship. We've been together ever since.''

Drew took a deep breath. ''I didn't mean to go on, but I wanted you to know a little bit about him before tonight. He's a sophomore at the university, and I'm really proud of him. He's making good grades. One reason I told you this is that Jesse doesn't relate well to women—most likely because his mother abandoned him. After all these years, he's even reserved around Consuela. If he ignores you, don't take it personally.''

After Drew left, Sunny reminisced for several minutes, wondering if things could have been different—for Drew, for both of them—if things would have been different for them if they'd had more time together before he'd refused to see her, before his bitterness had become so ingrained.

The three men sat in the bare room. An armed guard stood at the door. A clock, high up on the dingy gray wall, ticked loudly, counting the few minutes allotted them.

Rob looked around. He felt a chill that came from the atmosphere rather than the temperature of the place. This was his first visit, and he was glad to have a minute to adjust to the scene while Gus quietly fired questions at Mason. He hadn't seen Gus since he'd been sent up, but Gus had told Mason to bring him today.

Rob had been following the instructions he'd been given. He'd secured the job at the lieutenant's ranch.

"Your extracurricular activities?" Gus asked.

"Up and growing—probably five or six inches high."

Gus nodded. "Like I've said before, size isn't so important, just the evidence of what the lieutenant does with his free time nowadays. Sure too bad when a good cop turns."

Gus turned toward Rob. According to Mason, the boy had done well—hardly a boy anymore at the age of twenty-six, but he supposed he'd always think of him that way. They'd taken a chance on Robbie, but he'd been the best option for the ranch.

"Rob. Any problems with the new job?"

"No problems. Did you get the newspapers I sent?"

"Yeah. Very interesting. The hotshot lieutenant may have another weak spot besides the druggie. You were using your head, sending them without a return address. Is she there at the ranch, Robbie?"

"That's what the little kid says."

"Do you have all the ingredients you need for the brownies?"

Robbie nodded, smiling.

"Good. Should be about time for one of the kid's visits."

FIVE

Catching her breath, Sunny sat propped on the edge of the bed and rubbed her underarms. The crutches simply didn't work. She'd shown other people how to use them, even tried them herself a few times with two good legs, but this was entirely different. Failure had never been a word she'd used in regard to herself, and she'd be hanged if two configurations of wood would add it to her vocabulary at this point in her life.

It was still early in the afternoon. Determined to go under her own steam to the table for the family dinner tonight, she once again reached for the crutches that leaned against the bed. One of them slid sideways, clattering onto the oak floor, and the other one followed after its mate, echoing the racket.

Perched on the satin comforter, Sunny blew on her bangs, cooling her heated skin. She looked down at the crisscrossed crutches, contemplating how she could retrieve them without losing her balance. Unable to put her left foot on the floor, her right, sock-covered foot lost its tentative grip and she slipped to the floor just as she heard the door open.

Drew stood with his back against the closed bedroom

door. He'd been across the hall in his den when he'd heard the clatter. He knew what the noise meant. He couldn't prevent the smile that covered his face. Sunny grinned impishly.

Drew walked toward her, never taking his gaze from her flushed face—whether from exertion or embarrassment, he didn't know. He only knew how beautiful she was. He knelt between her outstretched legs. Without thought, he reached out to touch her face. The backs of his fingers caressed her cheek.

She was fast becoming a ray of sunshine—no, he corrected himself, a distraction; one he didn't want, and one he didn't need in his orderly life. The coolness of the cast beneath his other hand pulled his wandering thoughts back. His voice held a rough edge. "Did you hurt your ankle?"

She didn't answer but continued to look at him with rounded eyes. "You hit with quite a thump, but it didn't look like your leg did anything other than slide out in front of you."

"You saw the *whole* thing?" She grimaced in self-disgust.

"When I heard the first crutch hit the floor, I was on my way. I watched you slide off the bed and onto the floor—quite gracefully, I might add. I didn't know you were going to try using the crutches today. Why didn't you ask for help?" He raised the slash of his dark brows.

"I didn't see any reason not to use them since my hand is healed. I'm tired of being confined to that chair."

Drew studied her from his position on the floor, recognizing the determined glint in her eyes. Lifting her left hand, he turned it over and gently rubbed his thumb over the reddened scar. The burns had looked much better this morning.

"You're going to have to go easy on this hand, you

know." His voice had suddenly become a hoarse whisper.

She looked down and watched Drew rub his thumb over the red scar that crossed the center of her palm. Her hand tingled in an odd sort of way.

"Sunny?"

He seemed oblivious of where he was kneeling—between her thighs. Sunny had never been more aware of a man than she was at that moment, but then, she'd never been so conscious of her own body, either. When had this happened—this acute awareness? *This* awareness wasn't only of Drew, *this* awareness was of them together—a couple—male and female. His closeness caused a frantic fluttering in her heart. She could barely hear the words he was speaking over her own rushing thoughts.

"Sunny?"

She glanced up at him. "Hm?"

"Your hand." Drew grazed his thumb over the tender skin again. "You need to be careful and not overdo it."

"I will. I can't get the hang of these crutches. I know how they're supposed to work, but I can't coordinate them."

He nodded in understanding. "Let me help you up."

With his hands under her full breasts, he lifted her. Pure sensation rushed through Drew and, to his utter chagrin, landed with obvious energy in the crotch of his already too tight jeans. He'd frighten her into heart failure. He closed his eyes and tried to step back. Her hands curled into his shirt. He took a deep breath. He opened his eyes and looked at her. Eyes, slumberously soft, were focused on his mouth.

His breath lifted her wispy bangs as he brushed his lips across her forehead. Her delicate scent was exactly as he remembered it. This was the woman he remembered from the hospital, the one from his dreams. It wasn't perfume. This was Sunny. Heat torched his body. Her hands trembled between them.

Didn't she ever wear a bra? He didn't *need* her. He did. He wanted her—more than he believed possible. He took a deep, shuddery breath. She felt so good, so warm. She fit perfectly against him. A virgin! And he needed her for his very own.

Even as he uncompromisingly shoved Sunny away in his mind, his gaze instinctively dropped to her lips. Soft, sensuous lips. Lips bare of anything but natural color. Lips parted and moist from the tip of her tongue, which peeked from between her teeth. Lips that begged for his.

Like a purring feline, her fingers softly kneaded his shirt, catching the hair on his chest. He refused the artless and, he was certain, unconscious temptation she so innocently offered. He frowned. Was it innocent? Drew lifted his gaze to her eyes. Desire—pure desire filled them.

Sunny felt the back of her knees touch the edge of the bed. Her arms wedged between them, she felt safe even though she was trapped between the bed and Drew's hard body. She couldn't have moved if her life depended on it. But why would she want to? This felt wonderful—no, that wasn't the feeling. With a funny little noise, her breath caught in her throat.

She watched as the color of his eyes darkened. His hands felt like a brand under her breasts. She felt her nipples bud against the satin of her chemise. His lips across her forehead felt like velvet. As he pulled back, his breath fanned her face. He stared at her lips. She glanced down at her hands, which seemed to have a will of their own. If only his shirt were unbuttoned. She wanted to touch him.

Her gaze wandered up the column of his throat to his mouth. She wanted to circle his neck with her arms, and pull him close—close enough to kiss, close enough to touch the hardness of his desire she'd briefly felt before he'd edged away from her body. Desire, *that* was what she was feeling.

Where was his willpower? He'd always prided himself on his restraint in every area of his life. Drew swore silently even as he made a tentative pass with his mouth across her lips. At the soft sound from her throat, he murmured, ''Open your mouth for me, Sunny.''

She denied him nothing; he gave and he took the pleasurable sweetness of her mouth. There was no hesitancy now. Their lips met and mated. His hands rushed down her back and gripped her hips, holding her tight against his desire.

He released her, his breath rushing in and out of his heaving chest. He traced her swollen lips with this thumb. Clearing his tight throat, he let loose of her as if she were a red-hot coal.

Sunny had no choice but to release the cotton shirt, which had wrinkled under her touch. Robbed of his heat, she wanted it back. Sunny cocked her head to one side as she studied him. She saw only the gentle man with the tender touch—not his core of steel with the tough, defensive attitude, not the cynical look that now flashed in his dark eyes.

Avoiding Sunny's hot, appraising gaze, Drew leaned over and picked up the crutches, propping himself up on them. His composure recovered, he looked at Sunny again, then glanced out the window when he saw the determined tilt of her chin.

Sunny stared at his mouth. It no longer looked stern and unforgiving, but soft and sensuous. Softly she said, ''I knew it could be good between us.'' A secret smile twinkled in her eyes.

His glance darted to her face. One of the crutches fell with a thud against the bed, narrowly missing her leg. Her smile scared him more than her determination.

He picked up the crutch that had fallen onto the bed beside her, leaned them both against the wall, and walked toward the door. He left the room with the soft click of the door.

Lowering herself onto the bed, she smiled and touched her lips. Moments later she fell asleep.

Two hours later, Sunny still relished the feel of his mouth on hers. For a few minutes his control had disappeared along with the cynicism that seemed to ride on his shoulder like the monkey on an organ grinder's back. She wasn't adept at this sexual chemistry thing, but she wasn't daft either. He'd wanted her.

Now she was rushing. Waving the hair dryer over her damp hair with one hand, she applied lip gloss with the other. Balancing on one foot, she stood before the mirror in a French-cut teddy. A smile tugged at her lips at the thought of him handling this very item when he'd packed her clothing.

She'd given up on the idea of using the crutches, because her hand was too tender and she wanted to wear a new jewel-colored caftan. If she attempted to use the crutches, the long, flowing skirt would most likely get tangled up and she'd go sprawling. Once today was enough, although the consequences had been most rewarding. She slipped the dress over her head. The soft, silky fabric slid over her body. The mandarin collar graced her slender neck, and the neckline was slit to just above her breasts. She looked in the mirror at her image, and liked what she saw.

It might pay to appear feminine and a little helpless tonight. She knew nothing about flirting, nothing about getting a man's attention, but she had the instinctive feeling that the direct approach wouldn't work. If only she had experienced these matters of the heart before. But inexperienced or not, it was full speed ahead.

Sunny rolled the chair into the hallway. Her confidence dwindled sharply as she heard voices, but she slowly continued in the direction of the sound. She wished she'd been able to use the crutches so everyone wouldn't be looking down at her, but this was better than falling on her face.

Sunny sat in the doorway of the living room and watched as Drew and Mike stood by the fireplace talking with a slender, curly-haired young man. Jesse, she assumed. They joked and laughed, unaware of her presence. She felt like an eavesdropper. She wished she'd stayed in her room or gone on to the kitchen.

Quickly coming to a decision, she started to back out of the room just as Rico rushed up behind her, giving her a push. Sunny's backward motion and Rico's forward motion caused the rubber wheels to screech on the oak floor and the chair to jerk, almost throwing her out of the seat. Color tinged her cheeks. She certainly had everyone's attention now.

"What an entrance, Sunny," Mike hooted as he came forward to give her a bear hug. "You look great. Gorgeous. A lot of color in your cheeks. Looks like Drew's been taking good care of you." He winked and grinned broadly. Noticing Sunny's blush deepen, Mike glanced at his scowling brother.

Though she felt embarrassed, she couldn't keep the quick laugh at bay. She'd missed Mike and his humor.

Sunny shook hands with a suddenly quiet and subdued Jesse. As the gossip and chatter between her and Mike died down, Sunny glanced around at the four males, feeling bewildered by the awkwardness that now filled the room. Then understanding clicked—Jesse felt ill at ease with her there, and it seemed to pass right on to Drew and Rico, too.

The sudden interruption of Consuela entering the living room and giving orders for everyone to come to dinner gave Sunny a moment to collect her usual poise.

"Dinner's on the table. The pot roast is perfect. Don't let it get cold. Sunny, you look ravishing."

Consuela started pulling one of the dining room chairs away from the side of the table. "You sit here by me, Sunny. Us women got to stick together."

Before Sunny realized what was happening, Mike picked her up and put her down on the wooden chair.

Dinner was delicious and the conversation varied, but Sunny had only one focus. With lowered lashes, she watched Drew. She was impressed by his rapport with Jesse and Rico. His love for them was obvious. And Jesse obviously had the utmost respect for Drew. He seemed quite open about what was happening in his life at the university. Jesse gently teased Rico and occasionally lightly cuffed him in affection. But, as Drew had warned, Jesse acted as though Sunny didn't exist. His discomfort was obvious. He'd mumbled a quiet greeting and had avoided looking at her since, even though he sat directly across the table from her.

Sunny responded to a few questions Mike asked, but her gaze continually strayed, as did her thoughts, to the man at the head of the table. Drew, however, seemed intent on looking at anyone but her. She'd tenuously sought his attention several times, but to no avail.

After dinner, Mike wheeled her into the living room and toward the fireplace. Handing her a mug of coffee, he sat in a nearby chair. "Games, Sunny?" Leaning forward in the chair, he said, "I would have never believed it possible if I hadn't seen it with my own eyes. There are probably at least fifty men back in the city who would savor watching you seek a man's attention."

"Stuff it, Mike. You don't know what you're talking about," she hissed as Mike leaned back in his chair.

"That color in your cheeks certainly isn't windburn. What's been happening up here? A little hanky-panky?

I'd say that would be a little tricky with that heavy cast on.''

What could she say? That she was falling in love with Drew?

Drew glared at Sunny and Mike as he came into the room, not caring if anyone noticed his irritation. Sunny and his brother spoke in shorthand, understanding each other easily. They were politely rude to each other as only close friends could be. He couldn't hear what they were saying, but as close together as they had their heads, it couldn't help but be of a private nature. He'd never really understood their relationship.

She was worming her way under his strongest defense. Until this afternoon, Drew was certain she'd been unaware of him as a man. It was as though a switch had been flipped on inside her. Instead of lingering, instead of playing with fire, instead of kissing her as though his life depended upon it, he should have helped her up and left the room. Frustrated at his wandering thoughts, he glanced at the pair at the other end of the room.

Without a shadow of a doubt, Drew knew that Sunny had dressed with a purpose. With her every movement, he'd wondered which piece of silk she had on underneath that thing she was wearing. She wanted him to notice her. He had.

Was she planning to test her virgin wings on him while she had nothing else to occupy her time? He refused to be a cure for any woman's boredom. He hated that he'd been aware of every bite she'd taken and every word she'd uttered during dinner. If only he could have a short fling with her. Then maybe he could rid himself of the tantalizing image that continued to disturb him.

It was almost midnight. Drew stood out on the deck of the master suite, a snifter of brandy in his hand.

He'd thought everyone had gone to bed. He was wrong. He could hear Mike's and Sunny's voices as they drifted up from the room below. The happy sounds grated on his nerves like fingernails repeatedly screeching across a chalkboard. He could vaguely remember a time when he had looked at life as simply as Sunny and Mike seemed to, but that was more years ago than he wanted to count.

He knew his life had been painted with a different brushstroke from theirs, and the color was dark and textured. He'd seen so much of the seamy side of life in his work. He'd seen some of the worst in people, but then, so had Mike and Sunny in their work.

Since his accident, he realized his view of himself had changed drastically. He refused to allow himself to think of marriage. How could he? There were so many basic things in life he couldn't do anymore. He couldn't think of asking a woman to share his limited life-style.

For the last two years, he'd had an ongoing relationship with a friend in Santa Fe. Sylvia was an attorney, and her life centered around her career. They understood each other—giving and getting without the commitment neither one of them needed. The relationship filled a need for each of them. It had been quite a while since he'd seen Sylvia. He'd give her a call.

The next afternoon, Sunny sat at the kitchen table watching Consuela make tortillas for dinner and scanning the newspaper. The teakettle began whistling. Drew, Mike, and the boys, as Consuela referred to them, had gone horseback riding early. They were back from their ride, but Sunny hadn't seen any of them since last night.

As the housekeeper brewed tea, she said, "Drew, Mike, and Rico went over to the neighbor's ranch to see their new colt. One of our stallions is the sire, so everyone is interested."

"I didn't realize this was a working ranch."

"Drew owns a lot of land. It's actually half Mike's, too. Most of the land is leased out, though. Drew only uses a small portion for his breeding operation."

Every day she learned more about Drew. Sunny didn't think he tried to be secretive. He simply didn't talk about himself, at least not to her. A rare breed for certain. In her experience, most men loved to talk about themselves to anyone who would listen.

The back door slammed, interrupting their conversation. "What's for dinner?" Jesse asked as he opened the refrigerator door and peered at the contents. "I'm starved," he added as he grabbed a bowl. He swung the door shut and reached for a spoon from the drawer. Jesse pulled out a chair, slouched in it across the table from Sunny, and began to eat something that resembled cold stew.

With his mouth full and looking directly at her, he asked, "So, how's your ankle, Sunny?" But before she could answer, he jumped up from the table and grabbed an apple from the basket on the counter, threw it in the air, and caught it. He sat back down in the chair and bit noisily into the fruit.

Sunny squinted. Was this Jesse? The same serious young man she'd met last night? She glanced over at Consuela and noticed she had a look of utter confusion on her face.

Hands on her hips, Consuela asked, "You okay, Jesse?"

"Doin' great. Charlie and I had a super afternoon. The new guy he hired a while back is really neat. He's been everywhere and done about everything imaginable. Said his cousin had been at Woodstock. Can you believe that? He's a great cook, too. Baked some fantastic brownies. Course, Charlie couldn't have any 'cause he's diabetic, so I ate his share, too."

Jesse stood up and walked over to where Consuela

was making the tortillas. "These look really good."
He reached for one she'd just taken off the griddle.

"Those are for dinner," Consuela muttered as she
swatted at his hand. "Are you sure you're all right?"

He laughed loudly. "Never been better." Whistling,
Jesse pushed through the kitchen door.

Sunny had enjoyed the weekend and all the activity
that surrounded it—not only Mike's company, but the
whole new side of Drew she'd seen. However, she was
more than ready to have a little time to herself with
him.

She sat sleepily in an overstuffed chair in the living
room with her legs propped on an ottoman. She loved
this room with the roaring fire and its relaxed
atmosphere.

Drew and Mike were watching a football game on
the big-screen television. Watching was a mild word
for the loud criticism they shouted. Their favorite team
was losing, and they offered graphic suggestions to the
coach. At the opposite end of the room, Rico dueled
with the underworld in his favorite computer game, and
Prince slept by the flagstone fireplace.

During a time-out, Mike stood and stretched. "I've
got to get going. I've got a dinner date tonight."

"Anyone I know?" Sunny asked.

"Um, I don't think so. She's fairly new at the
hospital."

"No need to ask if she's pretty, but give her my
sympathy," Sunny teased.

Mike laughed before asking, "Anybody know where
Jesse is? No? If you see him, tell him we need to
leave."

A few moments later, Jesse wandered into the room.
Without glancing away from the television, Drew commented, "You need to get packed. Mike wants to leave

fairly soon.'' He looked over at Sunny as he added, ''He's got a date with a new girl tonight.''

Sunny didn't hear a word Drew said. Her eyes narrowed and she sat motionless, watching Prince. The dog had gone from a sleeping position to an alert one. He sat at Jesse's feet and his paw hit the plastic bag that hung from Jesse's hand, causing it to swing against the young man's leg. Two sharp barks followed.

Wide-awake, Sunny asked, ''What's in the sack, Jesse?''

''Brownies. The new guy Charlie hired made them. I had some yesterday. They're really good.'' Jesse reached down and patted the dog. ''What's the matter, Prince? You like chocolate, too?''

In answer, the dog batted at the sack again, growled, and sat back on his haunches.

Sunny glanced at Drew, who continued to be oblivious to anything but the game. But Mike stood rooted at the foot of the stairs, watching Prince intently.

''Call off your dog, would ya, Sunny?'' Jesse asked as he raised the bag above Prince's reach.

''Jesse, could I have one of your brownies?'' Sunny asked.

Without looking away from the game, Drew answered absently, ''If you're still hungry, Sunny, I'm sure Consuela has something in the kitchen. But don't take the poor kid's care package. It's tough eating cafeteria food all the time.''

''I'm not hungry, Drew. I want to see what has Prince so upset.'' Sunny looked at Mike, who had come a little farther into the room. Mike, a frown on his face, shook his head at Sunny. She spoke in a commanding voice to the dog, but it took a second command to bring him to her side. She looped her fingers under his leather collar as Jesse dashed up the stairs.

Leaning back in the chair, she held on to the dog's collar. She filtered through her memory, trying to recall everything she'd been told about Prince's training. Mike's attention was back on the game, but she'd known by the look on his face that he had drawn the same conclusion as she had about the brownies. He'd evidently dismissed the possibility just as quickly. If Drew would take his eyes off the game for a minute, he would know what was happening. He hadn't been out of touch for that long.

Tension gripped her, and Prince whined as her fingers clenched into a fist, tightening his collar even more. "Sorry, boy." Sunny removed her fingers from the collar and gently petted the dog's head. She didn't hear the end of the game or see Drew touch the remote control to turn off the set.

Before she could stop him, Prince trotted over to Jesse, who stood at the foot of the stairs. Once again the scene played out. This time Jesse shoved at the dog with his leg when Prince sniffed at the duffel bag. Prince latched on to the strap.

"What's with your dog? He seems to have a problem. I thought he wouldn't go for food," Drew said.

Before Sunny could answer Drew, Mike had pulled the dog away from Jesse and firmly taken him by the collar back to Sunny's side. Again she held Prince by his collar.

Mike braced himself on the arms of the chair and said quietly, "Don't jump to any conclusions or say anything rash, Sunny." He said a little louder, "I'll call you."

Mike hustled Jesse out the door, and Drew followed them outside. Stranded, Sunny sat in the big chair. Her wheelchair was across the room where Rico had left it earlier after practicing wheelies before he had gotten involved in the computer game.

Prince woofed softly and laid his head on her knee. He seemed as confused as she was.

Drew returned a few minutes later. His hands fisted

on his hips, he asked, "What was that all about anyway? Your dog was going to have Jesse's brownies or burst. Isn't Rico feeding him enough, or does he simply have a penchant for chocolate?"

"Prince doesn't eat chocolate, Drew. He's been trained to sniff out certain things."

When Drew tilted his head to the side and looked at her as if she were one brick short of a load, Sunny paused, then took the plunge. "Cannabis, Drew."

SIX

The word hit Drew like a sledgehammer between the eyes. He flinched. *Cannabis*. He turned around and walked over to the window, rubbing his hand over his face. Except for the muted sounds of Rico's computer game, the room was silent, yet it screamed with tension. "Damn it, Sunny! You and your dog are crazy. Impossible, it's impossible."

Sunny loved his normally soft, velvety voice. This was the first time she'd ever heard him raise it, and the sound grated on the guilt she felt. She should have held her tongue.

Pushing the ottoman from underneath her feet, she glanced at the wheelchair and knew there was no way to reach it herself. She watched Drew's back. The muscles in his shoulders alternately contracted and bunched as he dragged his fingers through his hair. His obvious turmoil pulled her like a powerful magnetic force. She wanted to go to him, to massage the tension from his shoulders, but she sat stranded without her wheelchair.

"Do you have any idea what you're claiming? Do you, Sunny?" he asked quietly from his position by the window. Drew was surprised his voice didn't quaver.

When she didn't answer, he came around and stood in front of her. "It's just not possible. You don't know Jesse like I do. If you did, you'd realize how ludicrous your accusation is. He's been clean for almost three years. Three years! He wouldn't. I know he wouldn't. Damn it, those were brownies that dog was after, Sunny. Brownies."

"Rico? Rico!" Drew hollered again before he had the boy's attention. "Have you been feeding this dog like you're supposed to?"

"Yeah, Dad. Every night just like Sunny told me to. I didn't forget, honest."

Drew shot one last glare at her before he strode from the room. Sunny listened as he shut the door of his den. She couldn't have shocked him more if she'd struck him over the head with a billy club. Sunny had no idea how long she sat in the chair mulling over all of the possibilities, but she did know she had to speak to Drew.

"Rico? Rico!"

"Why's everybody yelling at me today? I haven't done anything wrong."

I'm sorry. I didn't mean to yell. Could you please bring the wheelchair? Then you can go back to your game."

Rico walked across the room and hopped in the chair. He gunned it across the room like a race car driver at the Indy 500. Rico held the chair while she levered herself onto the seat.

"Thanks. You're a great kid."

"I'm tired of playing anyhow. I think I'll take Prince out and play Frisbee, and then I'll feed him. I *have* fed him every night, just like you told me."

"You've done great. Prince will be your friend for life."

"I wish Prince could stay here forever," Rico said as he scratched the dog behind the ears. When he glanced up at Sunny, he added in almost a whisper, "You, too, Sunny."

If she could have gotten away with it, she would have given him a hug, but Sunny settled for a ruffling of his hair. If only Drew would offer the same invitation. She swallowed the lump that had formed in her throat.

Deep in thought, Sunny slowly wheeled herself down the hall, the wheels making a soft squeak on the polished oak floor.

Could she be wrong? It was a little late for doubts, she reminded herself. As far as she knew, neither Mike nor Drew had seen Jesse yesterday after he had eaten the brownies. His expansive mood in the kitchen had been a total reversal from the first night, and then last night he'd been almost morose. She also knew from Consuela's confusion that this was abnormal behavior for Jesse.

Mike had known exactly what she'd been thinking. Their minds had clicked with the same conclusion. So why had he signaled for her not to say anything? Yet she'd gone full steam ahead and blurted out her unfounded notion. She wanted to be wrong, but if she was right, wouldn't Drew want to know?

Mike had said he would call. Was he going to check out one of those brownies? Talk to Jesse? She should have waited.

She had angered Drew. With a single word, she'd ripped apart the little rapport that had built between them. The last thing she wanted to do was hurt Drew for any reason. Sunny wondered if there was any way to repair the damage. She paused at the door of Drew's den. After wiping her damp palms on the leg of her pants and taking a deep breath, she slowly turned the doorknob and pushed open the heavy door.

The dusk of evening cast deep shadows, but she could see him well enough. Though Drew's den was located directly across the hall from her bedroom, this was the first time she'd been in it. With a cursory glance she noted the wall of books, the computer desk, and the leather couch, but her gaze riveted on Drew. His feet were propped up on an antique rolltop desk of golden oak. His leather chair was tipped back, his eyes were closed, and except for his steepled fingers, he appeared totally relaxed.

Sunny looked at him for several moments, absorbing every nuance, staring to her heart's content and loving what she saw. She would give anything for the freedom to go to him—to put her arms around him, to absorb his hurt and his frustration for her own. But that privilege did not belong to her. She was also sure any empathy she offered would be rebuffed. Did he confide in anyone or did he keep his own counsel? With a frustrated shrug she concluded he was asleep and reached to pull the heavy door shut.

Drew had heard her wheel to a stop outside the door of his den. With half-closed eyes he'd watched the doorknob turning, he'd seen her glance around the room, but he'd *felt* Sunny's detailed perusal of his body.

She hadn't even bothered to knock. He'd thought if he pretended to be asleep, she'd be polite enough to leave. But no, not Sunny. He'd kept his distance from this woman. He'd only touched her to change the dressing on her injured hand.

Until yesterday, that is, when the concept of distance had been shattered—when he'd picked her up off the floor, when he'd followed up on a small part of his fantasy. Sunny's nearness, the scent of her, the taste of her, the softness of her body under his hands, had tipped the scales. Now he didn't know if he could regain his balance. Hell, he was beginning to think his need of her was fundamental to his existence.

To think he'd actually believed her when she'd said

she wouldn't intrude in his life. He wanted her sunshine. He resented her—her invasion into his life, into his privacy. He had no need of her—none whatsoever—and he'd continue to tell his body that as long as necessary. Frustration and anger gnawed deeply, with other emotions he couldn't as easily identify.

The wheel on Sunny's chair squeaked on the oak floor, and before he could check the impulse, his boots hit the floor with a loud thud. He sighed, "Do you need something, Sunny?"

She'd come out of concern for Drew, yet ended up getting caught staring at his body. "I shouldn't have intruded. I won't disturb you any longer."

"Stay!" When he realized how rude the command sounded, he added, "Please. I want to talk to you."

With a nod of acceptance, Sunny moved into the room. Drew stood up and went to shut the door before he turned back toward her. "Do you seriously think there could be marijuana in those brownies?"

She took a deep breath. "I honestly don't know. I do know Prince went through the entire training program for police work before he was taken out of the program because he got carsick too often, and always if it was hot. I've watched demonstrations with dogs, and I've seen it work once. That dog's reaction was identical to Prince's. You've worked with dogs, haven't you?"

"Yes, but I wasn't really aware of what was going on this afternoon. I was absorbed in the game."

Sunny watched Drew as he paced several times between the windows and the opposite wall of bookshelves before she suggested, "Drew, there's always the possibility Jesse didn't know what the brownies contained. He may be an innocent victim of a cruel prank." Drew stopped pacing and began to listen. "Do you know the man who gave them to him?"

"We hired the guy a few weeks ago. I ran a check

on his references, and I checked to see if he had a police record of any kind, but he came up clean. I think Prince was wrong this time."

She was about to put her foot in her mouth again, but he had the right to know. "Drew, there's one other thing I think you should know about. Something rather strange happened yesterday afternoon in the kitchen when Consuela was making dinner."

Drew listened in disbelief as Sunny related what had transpired. "Jesse was really impressed with this guy. His cousin was at Woodstock. Maybe he always bakes brownies that way. You know how some people have a very casual attitude toward the use of marijuana."

The oath that followed was neither mild nor soft this time. "If there was marijuana in those brownies, it could send Jesse into a relapse."

"I know that. I'm also hoping Prince made a bad call."

Drew's snort of disgust had Sunny stiffening her spine.

"I'm going over to the bunkhouse and find out what's going on. I'll see if I can find out what this guy is up to."

"Would you at least consider taking Prince with you?"

When Drew opened the door, Prince was sitting in the hall, his tail thumping as if in anticipation of the coming confrontation.

"Where's his leash? I might as well find out what he's capable of."

Gus glowered at Rob. "Tell me what happened."

"Yeah, Yeah. The lieutenant no less. He came out to the bunkhouse asking about brownies. Can you believe it? The kid must've told him what a great cook I am."

When his older brother didn't appreciate his joke, he

went on. "He brought a dog with him. A shepherd—full-grown. I hadn't seen him before." His thoughts trailed off as he recalled the dog's reaction to him, and he still couldn't figure out why the dog hadn't gobbled up the steak he'd offered him this morning. He thought for certain he could win the dog over. But big brother didn't need to know everything that went on.

He was glad he had the ranch job. It was a lot easier than Mason's job—camping out and tending to the lieutenant's pot.

"And?" When his brother still didn't answer, he asked, "Were you ready?"

"Damn right I was. Offered him a brownie," he laughed. "I was real nice to the hotshot lieutenant. I saw him take a bite of it and carefully tuck some into his jacket pocket. I could have finished him off right there. Sure would have felt good."

"Don't even think of taking matters into your own hands, Robbie, or you'll have me to deal with. Keep to your business. Nothing else—nothing rash, nothing that isn't in the plan."

The sober look that had returned to the younger man's face was replaced by a cocky grin when his older brother asked, "You're sure he has no idea who you are?"

"Hell, no. How could he?"

Sunny sat on the side of her bed. Where was everyone? An agitated Prince had scratched on her door a few minutes ago. The light was on under the door across the hall, but even though she was curious as a cat about what had happened, Sunny didn't have the nerve to intrude again. The restless dog pacing the room now made her even more uneasy. Sunny slipped into bed, and breathing deeply to relax, she fell asleep just before the telephone rang across the hall.

*   *   *

Drew had hung up the phone over an hour ago, and yet he sat in the same position he had been in when the call had ended. At least he had a reprieve now. He'd be out of here before Sunny awakened in the morning. Even to himself, he sounded like a prisoner awaiting the opportunity to escape. He feared he was becoming a prisoner of his heart's desires. He knew what his body felt, and stubbornly conceded his heart wasn't far behind. Other than a short-term relationship, he had nothing to offer her, and he knew she would want more. Sunny would want *everything*. She was the type of woman who would settle for no less than a man's body *and* soul. Drew pushed away the thought that she would offer the same.

How could a woman be as aggressive as she was innocent? Was that possible? She was easy on his eyes, a thorn in his flesh, easy to talk to, a pain in the neck, hot to touch, a burr under his skin, and a growing cause of disruption in his life and heart. He needed to put some distance between them and gather his perspective. He shook his head, attempting to erase her image from his mind.

He had one more thing to do before he retired for what was likely to be another restless night. He called a friend on the force and asked him to run the name of the new hired man through a computer check. Prince had obviously been uneasy. The dog had wanted to investigate the room, and he'd had to be restrained with a tight grip on the leash. Drew wasn't ready to make accusations yet, but from Prince's behavior, he was sure there was something in the bunkhouse that shouldn't have been there.

Drew glanced at the piece of brownie in the plastic bag on his desk. He would drop it off in the lab—no, he'd leave early enough in the morning to wait for the results. Then he'd go on to his assignment.

*   *   *

Sunny gingerly eased down onto the kitchen chair as Consuela took her crutches from her and leaned them against the wall. As Consuela set her breakfast in front of her, Sunny asked without preamble, "Where's Drew? I need to talk to him."

"Aren't you feeling good? Should I call a doctor?"

"I feel fine. I just need to ask Drew about something."

"Oh, that's too bad. He ate breakfast about two hours ago and left."

Sunny glanced at her watch and realized it was only seven o'clock. "Left? When will he be back? At lunchtime?"

"He said not to expect him for a week." Noting Sunny's distressed look, she added, "But he always calls every evening to check on things when he's gone. Maybe you could talk to him then."

When the phone rang a few minutes later, Sunny listened carefully when Consuela answered. "Drew, Sunny and I were just talking about you. She asked for you this morning." After a short pause, she answered, "No, she's fine."

"I want to talk to him," Sunny interrupted, but Consuela was already hanging up the phone.

As the housekeeper eased herself into the chair across the table from Sunny, she said, "He was in a hurry, so he just wanted you to know that everything was negative, and for you not to worry. I don't understand what that means; do you?"

Sunny was slow to respond as she glanced out the window. "I'm not sure I do either." A week suddenly seemed like an eternity.

SEVEN

The sky had just begun to lighten when Sunny let Prince out the front door. Bored silly, she stood hunched over on her crutches and watched the split leg of her jogging pants flap silently as she swung her casted leg back and forth. With Drew away, time stood still.

Other than the muscle spasms in her calf that plagued her almost constantly, her ankle caused little pain. What she wouldn't give for a few miles of jogging in this cool mountain air. She did her best thinking then, and without the exercise, her thoughts were beginning to go in the same circuitous route until she felt an attack of vertigo would be a relief. The lack of exercise had provoked an irritability that was foreign to her and grated at her composure.

It had been five weeks since her accident. She had only three weeks in which to achieve her goal, and she was beginning to realize this goal might be significantly harder to attain than the others she'd accomplished so easily.

She'd searched her mind, knowing Drew was quite different from the man she'd envisioned as her mate for life, but in her heart Sunny knew they could be harmonizing counterpoints for each other's lives. He was strong, as strong-willed as she. And she'd learned he could be gentle—as gentle as he was strong.

Without a doubt, she knew she loved Drew. He was Mr. Right, her *personal* Mr. Right, and before too much more time lapsed, he would realize it also. The hunt was over. As the idea flitted through her thoughts, a bit of her confidence waned. He was certainly no Mr. Milquetoast, not that she'd want him to be. But with no experience, she'd need to keep her wits about her.

Her confidence returned. She was beginning to understand this goal was different. It included two people—two strong people—not just herself. This time there was an opposing force—Drew. She'd pursue him with a tenacious loving heart he wouldn't be able to resist. She'd never experienced such anticipation or such uncertainty.

With a heavy sigh, she turned from the window. Rico had talked to Drew last night. Drew's phone call had interrupted their game of Monopoly. When Rico had returned to the game, he could hardly contain himself. Drew would be home a day early.

Now it was only hours until his return—hours she needed to fill. Even though he'd called every evening, Sunny wasn't offered the chance to speak with him, and she had no idea what she would have said if she'd been given the opportunity. With an audible sigh, she turned to wander once more around her room before she headed toward the kitchen to make coffee. When she could even beat Consuela to the kitchen in the morning, her life was definitely missing something.

In the last few days, Sunny had prowled every nook and cranny of Drew's house—every part except the upstairs, where the master suite and two other bedrooms were located. She'd searched for hints of the real Drew, but she'd learned little. Several times during this week

she'd contemplated those stairs, and so far she'd decided against the risk of injury.

And, Sunny admitted to herself with a smile, even
worse than chancing injury was the idea of being plain
nosy, or at least of being found out. So why, instead
of going to the kitchen, was she now determinedly
bumping up the stairs on her bottom?

It was still dark, and only a small hanging lamp illuminated the stairwell. Sunny paused and looked down
at the crutches propped against the wall. If anyone came
by, she'd left a big hint as to her whereabouts. Why
had she given in to the impulse? She could have at
least left the crutches in her room and hopped on her
one good foot down the hall to the staircase. She was
shocked at her own rashness even as she continued her
slow but determined progress to the top step.

Feet straight out in front in her, Sunny leaned her
back against the wall and rested on the second-floor
landing. She was breathing a little faster than normal,
whether from the exertion or from what she was about
to do, she didn't know. She tugged at the split pant
leg, which had become twisted, and glanced around
trying to determine which room was Drew's.

As she pulled herself to a standing position, her foot
started to slip on the highly polished wood. Once again
she lowered herself to the floor and took off her right
sock, dropping it and leaving the other one on since
that foot always felt chilly. Pulling herself up, for what
she hoped was the last time, she made her choice.

Hanging on to the railing, she hopped off toward
what she concluded was the logical spot for Drew's
bedroom. Anticipation replaced the trepidation and the
slight amount of guilt that had previously forced her to
reconsider her actions.

Opening the door, Sunny reached around for the light
switch. With a soft click, two brass bedside lamps cast
soft lighting across the room. She clung to the door

casing as she stared. She didn't know what she'd expected, but this was not it. This room divulged a private part of Drew she'd found nowhere else in his home, not even in his den.

Personal mementos were everywhere. Family photographs and awards adorned the walls, along with what looked like an original Remington painting. A current best seller lay facedown on the bedside table, and she wondered why he hadn't taken it with him. The forest green comforter cast dark reflections onto the polished brass of what was obviously an antique bed.

Fascinated, Sunny hopped into the room and let the door shut behind her. She closed her eyes for a moment and breathed deeply. The scent was him. She wished she'd come up here every day. Hopping over to the bed, she sat down to rest for a minute before she explored further.

Before she quite knew what happened, Sunny had pulled his pillow out from under the comforter and rested her head on it. A contentment she hadn't felt in days brought a soft smile to her face as she tucked the pillow close against herself and let her eyes drift shut. Her dreams seemed a little closer. What would it be like to share this bed with Drew every night?

Exhausted but not sleepy, Drew pushed a hand through his rumpled hair and rubbed the back of his neck. He'd rushed through this assignment, finishing it ahead of schedule. And now he was hurrying home—dog-tired. Not wanting to spend another restless night, he'd packed and checked out of the hotel in the middle of the night.

Somehow he'd known he would push through this job in record time. He hadn't followed his usual pattern. He hadn't brought along the book he was currently reading, but then, it hadn't held his attention for several weeks now. He hadn't enjoyed the local scenery and food as he usually did. Drew had simply accomplished what needed to be done. This time he hadn't slept more than four or five hours a night, and that had been fitful even though he was exhausted. Although he'd learned years ago to fall asleep almost upon command, the ability had escaped him during the last few weeks. Getting away from Sunny had not changed that.

He'd gradually been adjusting to this different kind of job during the last year. It certainly couldn't compare to being out in the field, but it was still satisfying to know he helped educate the law enforcement agencies in how to control the drugs that seemed to invade even the smallest communities in New Mexico. He had loved his undercover work, but he again reminded himself that someone needed to do this job, and he was certainly qualified. Any state that bordered Mexico faced unique problems.

Anticipation kept his foot heavy on the accelerator. As he slowed to a stop by the side of his home, his heart thumped an extra time. He blinked and opened his eyes again. Under the illumination of the yard light, he saw Prince dashing toward the car. It was strange that he was out so early. The kitchen light wasn't even on yet. A glance at the digital timepiece on the dash told him it was a few minutes before five. Was something wrong? Even as the thought crossed his mind, he felt an unexpected tightening in his gut. He pulled a .45 automatic from a compartment in the car. He stepped out and glanced around before placing the pistol in the back waistband of his jeans.

Pain shot through his knee as he placed his weight on it. At the piercing reminder of his imperfection, he swore soundly and his shoulders straightened. Why had he hurried home? Why was he putting himself in this kind of no-win situation? When would he quit acting like a hormone-driven fool?

Prince seemed excited to see him, and by the coolness of his fur, he had been out for quite a while. He spoke quietly to the dog even as he scanned the surrounding area again. He was certain that if anything was wrong, Prince would warn him, but he still felt uneasy.

Tucking his fingers through Prince's collar, Drew glanced up at the house and frowned. It was dark—except for his bedroom. The drapes were drawn, but light shone through them. By the time he and Prince reached the front door, he'd worked some of the soreness out of his knee, and his limp had disappeared.

Everything seemed to be in order as he glanced into the living room and the kitchen. He turned the knob of Sunny's door in expectation of seeing her. He'd looked in on her when she'd first come to stay, but he'd stopped when each night it had become more and more difficult to leave the room after a quick check. On those nights sleep had eluded him.

At the sight of the rumpled but empty bed, his breath caught in his throat. Prince, however, didn't seem disturbed. Checking the bathroom, Drew retraced his steps. Starting toward the staircase, he saw the crutches propped against the wall, and frowned. Wherever she was, she was there under her own steam. The chair had been folded and pushed into a corner of her room.

Taking the stairs quietly, he and Prince reached the landing at the same time. A whine from the dog alerted Drew to the lone sock at the top of the stairs. Shaking his head, he stuffed it into his hip pocket.

A funny feeling, a mixture of fear and excitement, hit him. Avoiding the thought of what he was certain he would find, Drew checked the guest room first. In the next room he found Rico sound asleep, but Drew skipped the usual retrieving of the boy's blankets, which lay on the floor, and shut the door. That left only one possibility. Grasping the dog's collar, he went to the end of the hall and slowly opened the door to his own suite of rooms.

Drew forced a deep, shaky breath into his lungs. Leaning down, he softly commanded the dog to stay before he stepped into the room and closed the door in Prince's face.

She lay with her back to him, on her side, curled up in a fetal position except for the casted leg, which was thrown toward the middle of the bed. The whiteness of the cast stood out harshly against the green comforter. Exposed was a space of pale flesh where her shirt had separated from the pants.

Drew's immediate desire was to kneel beside the bed to taste her skin, to savor the softness of her back that seemed to beckon him, but he controlled his growing need even as his jeans seemed to shrink in size. Taking a few more steps into the room, he gripped the brass rail of the footboard and forgot the stern discussion he'd had with himself upon his arrival a few moments before. Her mouth was slightly parted, and he could hear the whisper of her deep breathing. His own pillow cradled her head as her arms clasped it to her breasts.

Drew's hands tightened as his one-way fantasy continued until he could feel the trembling of the brass rail beneath his fingers. He released his grip and scrubbed his face with his hands. Simply standing here looking at the sleeping woman caused his body to clamor for her. The trouble was, the woman in his bed wasn't just any woman. This was the woman who continued to threaten his sanity. This was Sunny. This was the woman who'd touched his heart three years before. He wanted to scream at her to get out. He wanted to lock the door and lie down beside her.

With one last glance, Drew turned and walked into the adjoining bathroom. His movements were mechanical as he took the pistol from his waistband, pulled out the clip, and slipped both into a drawer. He stripped, and ignoring the invitation of the Jacuzzi, he stepped under the cold, stinging spray of the shower. Gasping, he tried to clear his head, but it wasn't his head that needed clearing. It was his heart gone soft. A heart that constricted at the simple thought of her, let alone the sight of her in his room—in his bed.

The cold-water treatment did nothing except create an abundance of goose bumps on his overheated flesh. As he turned the water to hot, the auxiliary tank in the bathroom kicked in and gave him his wish, driving the tenseness from his tired muscles. Blanking his mind and banking the thoughts of Sunny, he concentrated on washing away the grime of the past twenty-four hours.

Wiping the fog from the mirror in the shower, he shaved the stubble from his face, then briskly dried himself before pulling on the thigh-length robe that hung on the back of the door. Drew stepped back into the bedroom as he tied the belt around his waist and walked over to open the drapes. Early morning sun brightened the room, but Drew was oblivious to its warmth and light as he gazed at the mountains. The whisper of a movement from the bed interrupted his reverie.

Sunny dozed between a light sleep and consciousness. Something was different. Something had awakened her, but she felt too good to open her eyes and look around. Breathing deeply, she inhaled a vaguely familiar scent before the reality of where she was hit her. Thank goodness no one had found her. She needed to get back downstairs before someone did, but she would lie here a moment more—just for one more dream-filled moment.

"Are we playing out the scene of Goldilocks and the three bears?" Drew growled.

As Sunny slowly rolled onto her back and opened her eyes, her conscious mind brushed away the fact that she was the intruder. With calm assurance, she stared at the man who faced her across the width of the bed. The top of his robe gapped, revealing dark swirls of hair. His hair was tousled and damp, his eyes wary.

She dropped her gaze to avoid answering his spoken question as well as the unspoken ones his eyes seemed to be asking. She quickly realized she should have kept her eyes in a safe place. His robe not only gapped at the top, but at the lower portion, also. She couldn't really see anything, but then again, not much was left to her imagination either.

"What kind of a game are you playing?" he asked evenly as he adjusted his robe. Heat washed up her body, and his eyes followed the rushing color flowing from her neck onto her face.

She watched him move around the end of the bed, and Sunny wished she'd gotten up and headed for the door about a minute ago, or better yet, that she had never ventured up here at all. Sunny shut her eyes as she felt his weight settle on the side of the bed. His hip and thigh flanked hers. Her eyes flew open as she felt his arms straddle her, dispelling any hope of escape.

She had dreamed of being this close to Drew, but his eyes did not hold the love she longed to see there. Instead, there was a silent dare Sunny felt inadequate to fulfill. Ignoring the challenge, she focused on the muscle that pulsed in his jaw.

In a quiet, velvety voice Drew asked, "What do you want, Goldilocks?" He reached up and touched her hair as he spoke. "You do remember the story of Goldilocks, don't you, Sunny? She got far more than she bargained for. She got the scare of her life and never ventured into the bears' bedroom again."

The lump in Sunny's throat, which she was unable to swallow, grew in size. She opened her mouth, but no sound escaped. Managing to pull her arms free, Sunny reached up to grasp the lapels of his robe. Instead, her fingers touched, then spread across, his chest. He was a mixture of textures and tantalizing scents. Warm skin and soft hair—soap, shampoo, shaving cream, some scent she couldn't place, but she knew this was Drew. Gradually her body responded. She'd waited all week for him—no, not all week, all of her life. Now he was here, close enough to touch, close enough to kiss, close enough to love.

His hand tugged hers from his chest and gripped it before loosening it to a caress. Sunny watched his eyes dilate and darken until they appeared black as he lowered his head toward her. She'd dreamed of this. Things were happening so quickly, she wouldn't even be breathless from this short chase, she thought as her eyes fluttered shut. Drew lightly kissed each eyelid and moved to nibble her ear. Sunny lifted her face, seeking his kiss.

He accepted her invitation. Drew lightly grazed his mouth across Sunny's—back and forth ever so slowly. She held her breath as he placed a soft kiss on each corner of her mouth, then nipped her bottom lip. With her gasp, he captured her mouth, tenderly exploring, catering to her growing desire. She threaded her arms around his neck and pulled him deeper into the kiss as her tongue began a hesitant foray with his.

His callused hands spanned her bare waist and moved up to brush the undersides of her breasts. She felt the cool air on her body as he lifted up the shirt to bare her breasts for his mouth. At the first flick of his tongue, a whimper escaped her throat, and with the next stroke, Sunny arched her back, begging for more. Her body was feverishly awash with sensations—sensations she couldn't identify but wanted more of. Hot sensations she was beginning to crave.

Drew's breath caught at the sight of her full breasts. Her nipples tightened under his gaze. On trembling arms, he lowered his mouth to worship, to feast on Sunny's soft, warm beauty.

With his first taste and Sunny's first whimper, Drew knew he could never get enough—his craving for her could never be sated. His hands roamed at will—pushing the top higher and then coasting down to slide the elastic waist of her pants lower. His mouth followed . . . his tongue circled her navel . . . his hands lifted her hips . . . his lips nibbled soft kisses lower, over the swell of her belly . . . he inhaled the feminine scent of her body . . . he wanted everything her eyes offered . . . he wanted her for life.

A distant sound slapped Drew with reality. He lifted his head a few inches. His arms shaky, his breathing labored, he listened, trying to identify the sound. A second later he heard Rico's boots on the stairs. Going down. His shoulders sagged and he let his head drop as he squeezed his eyes shut.

Sunny had stormed his defenses. He knew in his heart if he took this any further, if he took the taste of her into his mouth one more time, if he took the offer of her arched body, he would be making a commitment to her, a commitment he had no intention of fulfilling. If he so much as touched her again, there would be no turning back. As much as he wanted her, as much as his body demanded a hot haven within her body, Drew was determined not to make a place for Sunny in his life.

Yanking the shirt back down to her waist, he whispered, "Is this what you came up here for? A taste of lovemaking? Were you snuggled all warm in my bed hoping I would end your boredom? Why me, Sunny? Do you think because I'm a cripple, I can't get any other woman? Because I can't work on the force anymore, I'm an easy target? Why not pick on someone else? A man with two good legs. One that doesn't limp. I don't want your pity—or anything else from you."

Sunny watched as his eyes changed from the smoldering black of a moment ago to a cold, icy silver. She ached to take him in her arms and answer him with the three words that her heart was screaming—the three words that would explain everything to him—but her love found no voice. She searched his face, knowing he would not believe she loved him. Why was he taking something beautiful and soiling it with his cynicism?

"Don't ever come up here again. Whatever it is you're looking for, it's not here." He started to stand, and the sharp pain in his knee strengthened his resolve. He had a good life and he needed nothing more.

Drew watched her struggle off the bed and shakily hop toward the door. He wanted to take back the words he'd thrown at her. He longed to go to her, to continue their lovemaking. His jaw clenched tight, he turned his back to her. He denied himself. He denied Sunny.

Prince quickly jumped up as Sunny opened the door. She swallowed her tears as she bumped down the stairs, groped for her crutches, and placed them under her arms. The tears began as she neared her room.

She closed her bedroom door and locked it before she gave full rein to the choking sobs. At the side of her bed, she dropped the crutches on the floor, threw herself facedown on the rumpled sheets, and cried until her tears were gone and only the hollow sound of hiccups echoed in the room.

With her head still buried in her arms, she attempted to sort out what had happened. Drew had been exquisitely tender. Everything had been going beautifully—at least she'd thought so—when poof! He had pulled away. She'd been in too much of a daze to know if he had been as affected by their lovemaking as she had been. She longed for that intense pull of desire. She'd had another taste, and now her body demanded a three-course meal. Sunny sat up quickly to escape the poignant memory.

"What am I going to do now, Prince?" she whispered to the dog as she sat beside him. "Why did Drew push me away?" After a moment she continued the one-sided conversation. "He kept talking about his injury, about himself as if he was handicapped. No—crippled. This is the second time he's spoken of himself in that way. Does he really see himself that way? That somehow he's not a complete person? He might have won the first battle, but not the second."

She wouldn't hide. She had her pride, and he was not going to scare her away. She gave herself ten minutes to become presentable.

EIGHT

"What's the big occasion, Consuela? Company coming for breakfast?"

"No, I fixed a little extra for your homecoming. Sunny must still be in bed. Every day this week she's been up really early. Been out here almost before I can get the coffee brewed. You better check on her, Drew. Something might be wrong."

Drew ignored his housekeeper and continued to stare into his coffee cup as though it contained the answers to every problem in the world. A muscle jerked in his jaw.

Drew turned his head toward the door, listening. The sound of Sunny on her crutches grew louder.

"Good, she's up. Hold the door for her, will you, Drew?"

Sunny reached the kitchen and took a deep breath. The door opened. She stood face-to-face with Drew. She decided she must look worse than she thought when she saw his face pale, but he didn't look away.

"Good morning, Drew. I hope you had a successful trip."

Drew stepped back as Sunny started to come into the

room. She stopped at the place across the table from his spot and took the crutches out from under her arms.

Taking the crutches, Drew held Sunny's chair.

Consuela stood, her hands on her hips, looking from one to the other. "Sunny, you don't look too good. Are you all right?"

What he wouldn't give right now for a housekeeper who would mind her own business. It would be obvious, even to a man with poor eyesight, that Sunny had been crying. He was surprised she had the courage to come to breakfast at all.

"Will you serve breakfast, please?" Drew asked as he poured Sunny a cup of coffee from the carafe that sat nearby.

"Thank you." She hardly noticed the plate of food Consuela placed in front of her. Every nerve was alert to Drew.

She hadn't expected to meet him face-to-face, and she'd certainly not anticipated his obvious concern. His color seemed to be back to normal. He'd hardly touched his food, but then, she wondered if she'd be able to eat either.

Clearing her throat again, she asked, "Consuela, aren't you going to sit down and eat with us?"

Before Consuela could answer, the back door slammed and Rico and Prince rushed in. "Dad! You're home early." Rico threw his arms around Drew. "Wow! I've got tons of things to tell you."

"Wash your hands, Rico. You can talk to me while we eat breakfast together. I've missed you."

Sunny watched the interplay of love between the two before she glanced away. She wished she'd followed her first inclination and stayed in her room. She needed time to recover from the onslaught of emotions—he'd taken her from hot passion to cold despair. And now she felt numb. She also felt like an outsider looking in on a family scene of which she was no part.

Rico dried his hands on the towel and plopped in the chair between his dad and Sunny. He scooped a mouthful of eggs into his mouth and said, "Guess what! My scout troop is planning a camping trip in the spring. We have to earn badges on the trip, and our dads are supposed to come with us. Won't that be super?"

Sunny watched the odd play of emotions cross Drew's face before he answered Rico. "Sounds great, son."

"It's a backpacking trip. We're going to hike five miles and then pitch camp. We all have to carry our own gear. You'll come, right?"

Drew closed his eyes. How could he tell the child? Why did he have to have an audience? The kitchen had taken on an uncomfortable silence.

"Dad?"

Drew looked directly at Rico. "I'm sorry, really. I want to, but . . . I can't. You'll have to ask your uncle Mike to go with you."

"Why not? I want you to go. Uncle Mike's fun and all, but he's not you. It won't be the same if you don't go."

"My . . . I can't . . ." Drew closed his eyes against the pain and took a deep breath. "I won't be able to go with you because of my knee. We've talked about this before. I'd love to, but I can't hike like that anymore." Drew reached over and ruffled Rico's hair. "I'm really sorry, Rico."

"Yeah, I understand. I'll ask Uncle Mike next time I see him." Rico put his fork down. "I gotta get ready for school or I'll miss the bus."

Sunny couldn't swallow the bite of food in her mouth. She couldn't look at Drew either. Her heart went out to both of them. They were both hurting, and there wasn't a thing she could do about it.

"Consuela, could you check on Rico? Please," Drew asked.

Consuela glanced at the swinging kitchen door, then at Drew and Sunny. Placing the basket of muffins on the table, she left the room.

Sunny started to stand, but Drew interrupted her escape. "I need to talk to you a minute, Sunny."

Drew refilled their mugs with coffee. "I want to apologize for what happened this morning—in my bedroom."

Sunny's eyes met his in a rush. He hadn't meant what he'd said. Everything was going to be fine. The sparkle that he'd doused with his words this morning returned to her eyes, yet she noticed that his eyes appeared even colder than they had earlier.

"I shouldn't have touched you this morning. I had no right to take advantage of you . . . of the situation. You have my word it won't happen again."

Sunny stared at him. She refused to look away, and yet she wanted to hide in a small hole where he couldn't see her. Tipping back on two legs of his chair a little, Drew appeared to relax before her eyes. It was as if he'd done his duty, and now everything was back to his kind of normal. He took a sip of coffee and lifted his gaze to hers again.

"Just out of curiosity, what were you doing in my room? In my bed, to be precise?"

Color suffused her cheeks, but Sunny didn't flinch or look away. However, she did ignore Drew's question. "What happened on your bed this morning was beautiful, Drew. I do want it to happen again, and you can be sure it will."

The chair legs hit the floor with force. He didn't dare admit she was right. Drew leaned his forearms on the table and glared at her. This woman possessed the audacity of a foraging grizzly bear. "Damn you, Sunny."

Sunny had no idea how long it had been since Drew had stormed out the back door. She sat at the kitchen table, her fingers crumbling the muffin onto her cold omelet. The cheese had oozed and congealed into oily orange lumps on the plate. She brushed her hands over the plate, ridding them of the last crumbs, and picked up the mug with fingers that trembled slightly. After a quick sip, she put it down in distaste.

She'd been stunned by Drew's raging retort, and she still reeled from everything that had happened. But actually, the longer she thought about it, the better she felt. Sunny would be the first to admit to being a novice in the war between the sexes, but about the psychology of people, she was adept.

Could it be Drew was running scared? If he hadn't cared, if he hadn't been overtly rattled by her words, and if he hadn't appeared almost terrified, he would have had no reason to respond so vehemently. Most likely he would have laughed it off or even taken her up on her offer.

So this was going to be a chase after all—a spirited one at that. Only three weeks until she would be going home—that should be enough time. Giving him a little space in which to cool down might be a good idea, but it would have to be very little, because she refused to wait.

Drew and the stallion, Black Devil, thundered to the crest of the hill, both of them wet with sweat. He'd thought the exertion had cleared his head of the scent and the taste of the woman he'd found in his bed this morning, but the peace he'd so desperately sought evaded him. With sudden clarity Drew understood that, until he had the answer to the conflict within himself, until he could deal with his feelings for Sunny, he would find no peace. He was no closer to the answer to his dilemma than when he'd left well over an hour ago.

His body felt as though he had experienced every

emotion known to man in the last few hours. Coupled with the exhaustion of the last week, Drew readily admitted he was stressed, both physically and mentally. If he didn't gain control soon, he feared others would realize it shortly.

His emotional explosion with Sunny had driven away the last of his good sense. The leash on his emotions was frayed, stretching to the last thin thread. He knew he wasn't behaving in any manner close to his usual clearheadedness. Controlling the spirited stallion was taking every ounce of his strength, and he could feel his knee swelling from the pressure he had exerted to guide the horse. For a little while today he'd forgotten his knee could no longer tolerate the punishment of the ride he'd just taken without painful consequences. Drew swore again, and the stallion's ears lay flat as if he understood every word.

As Drew and the horse came to a halt before the barn, Charlie and the new hired man came out. Charlie frowned as he saw the lathered horse. "What in hell have you been doing?"

Drew glared at his foreman and then at the smirking man who stood beside Charlie. He'd forgotten. He'd planned to be out here early this morning to talk to Charlie about this man, Farley, and to search the bunkhouse. Even though the chemical contents of the brownie had been negative, he had an uneasy feeling from Prince's reactions that night. How could something so important have slipped his mind?

Drew grudgingly handed over the reins, knowing he would have his task cut out for him simply getting down off this horse, let alone rubbing down the beast. He glanced at the man beside Charlie and noticed the gloating sneer that Farley didn't attempt to hide.

Charlie looked to see what held Drew's attention. "You go on ahead to the tack room and get started, Rob," Charlie ordered the man. "I'll be along shortly."

Turning back to Drew, Charlie asked, "What's going on? I've never known you to bring a horse back in this kind of shape, and you look like hell, maybe worse."

Drew slowly slid to the ground, holding tightly to the saddle horn as inconspicuously as possible until he thought his knee could handle his weight. He stood drenched in sweat, his leg trembling.

Charlie's hand settled on Drew's shoulder. "Are you okay?"

Drew just shook his head. After a moment he said, "Take care of him for me. I didn't realize I was running him so hard. Thanks, Charlie."

Watching the ground under his feet to avoid stepping on a rock or an uneven area, Drew slowly made his way to the house. He'd get in the tub and soak it. A little ice would keep the swelling down in his knee. No one would ever have to know how stupid he'd been.

His hand clenched on the oak banister, he stared at the flight of stairs before him. He could have faced Mount Everest as easily. Taking the stairs one at a time, Drew used his good leg for leverage and then swung the other foot up and onto each stair, holding his aching knee straight. He hadn't hurt like this since the early days after his accident, nor had he been this stupid to push his luck with his knee—he knew only too well how unstable the joint was. Fear tightened his stomach. His progress was tedious. If he'd thought it wouldn't have invited the attention of the two women in the house, he would have sworn loudly and graphically as each step loomed before him.

A few minutes, but many silent curses, later, Drew sank into the swirling water of the Jacuzzi. Steam arose around him, creating his own private sanctuary where no one could intrude. As the knife-sharp pain in his knee diminished to a tolerable level, his thoughts began to race.

His mind cleared and he realized he'd made a critical tactical error with Sunny. Drew groaned aloud and sank farther into the deep tub. Losing his cool had been absolutely asinine. Damn! He had allowed Sunny to create an emotional whirlwind in the middle of his life.

Why hadn't he simply walked out of the kitchen? He could have pretended her suggestion hadn't fazed him. Why hadn't he acted as though the picture of her in his bed didn't send a rush of hot, pulsing blood? . . . He forced *that* thought away.

He hoped Sunny didn't have the savvy to understand why he'd responded as he did. His fists clenched under the water as her voice echoed in his mind, taunting him . . . *it was beautiful, it would happen again* . . . even as the intimate memory of her beneath him reverberated through his body.

Without thought for his knee, Drew jerked himself upright in the tub and stepped out. He promised himself that no matter what Sunny did or said from this moment on, he would not lose his temper. She would never see anything but the cool-cop image he had perfected years ago—the man who never got rattled, no matter what was going down.

He knew she would only be here three more weeks. Then his responsibilities would be over. Damn. If only Mike hadn't asked—if only he hadn't agreed. And he could also wish the image of her soft brown eyes and the silky halo of her hair hadn't burrowed in and lodged in his heart for the past three years. Now he'd added to the memories: the searing feel of her beneath him, her honeyed lips matching his in a heat he would never forget, her breasts responding to his touch. He didn't dare add even one more physical memory to his growing stockpile of fantasies.

Taking a deep breath, he ordered himself to calm

down. It really shouldn't be any problem to stay out of her way for three weeks, and when he couldn't avoid her, he'd act toward her in the same manner he did the housekeeper.

After drying himself, Drew leaned on the counter and propped his foot on the edge of the tub. This was the first time he'd really looked at his knee since his ride, and now he wished he hadn't. Seeing the amount of swelling seemed to increase the degree of his pain. He reached into the drawer for a pair of old athletic shorts and gingerly stepped into them before slipping into the robe that hung behind the bathroom door.

As he tightened the belt, the memories again began rolling like a slow-motion movie. Was it only this morning that Sunny had been here? He limped into the bedroom and stopped. The bed caught his gaze. The imprint of her soft, warm body was clearly defined. Turning his back, he slowly made his way toward the sitting area of his suite and lowered himself into the recliner. As he pushed back in the chair, he reached for the remote. Music filled the room. Drew shut his eyes and tried to relax.

Walking out of her bedroom, Sunny heard Consuela muttering as she came down the stairs, "Mercy, mercy, that boy's in bad shape. You should see his knee. It's really swollen. I've never seen him this way—not since he got out of the hospital. I don't mean just his knee. It's that temper of his. He doesn't use it very often, but when he does, it's time for me to get out of the way, quick. Most likely he'd even snap at a rattlesnake today. I've got to hurry. He wants an ice bag, pronto."

With lightning-quick decisiveness, Sunny propped her crutches against the banister. She lowered herself onto the first step, and for the second time that day, she began her backward ascent up the stairs. She had reached the last one when Consuela halted at the bottom with the ice bag in her hand.

"Psst. Consuela, I'm up here. Bring me my crutches, please."

The housekeeper clucked her disapproval and began climbing the stairs with the crutches clasped tightly in one hand and the ice bag hanging in the other. Panting, she reached the top. "What are you doing up here? You could get hurt. Then Drew would have my head on a platter." Consuela looked behind her and then asked, "How on earth did you get up here, anyway?"

"Sh. Sometime when we have nothing better to do, I'll show you. I thought I should check on him."

"I don't think he's going to like this idea, Sunny."

"I've been a nurse, remember?"

"I guess it'll be okay, but you holler if you need me."

"Everything will be fine; you'll see. You go ahead and do whatever it is you need to be doing."

Drew frowned and touched the volume control on the remote. Had he heard voices? Good thing he was on the second floor. Sunny wouldn't dare come up here again—not after this morning. Consuela should have returned by now with the ice bag. But after a moment, hearing nothing but the music, he increased the volume again. When he heard the knock, he frowned. "Consuela?"

Sunny reached for the doorknob with a determination she didn't feel. She was not here for herself. She was here out of concern for Drew. Music hit her with force as she opened the door. Even though she was a connoisseur of jazz, she didn't recognize the piece. What she did recognize was the stark loneliness that poured from the saxophone. If Drew's mood matched the music . . . Sunny glanced around, looking for Drew, but she didn't see him.

His voice reached her a second later. "Consuela! Have you got that ice?"

The voice was coming from an alcove on one side of the room. She could see part of a stereo unit, and bare feet propped on what looked like the footrest of a recliner. She hadn't even noticed that part of the room this morning. She glanced back and saw the housekeeper starting up the stairs again. Giving Consuela a quick thumbs-up sign, Sunny closed the door behind her. The ice bag swung from her hand as she entered the alcove.

Drew reacted as if hit with 220 volts. He pushed the recliner upright with a jolt and winced when his feet hit the floor. The loud wail of the sax throbbed around them, but his voice thundered even louder. "What the hell do you think you're doing up here?"

When he saw her lips move but couldn't hear her answer, he hit the power button on the remote, and the room was silent.

"I came to help."

"That's what I thought you said," Drew snapped. He'd already forgotten to keep his distance.

Sunny watched the storm in his eyes disappear, and that glacial color she hated took its place.

He spoke quietly. "That's very kind of you to offer, but I don't need any help. Just leave the ice bag and go."

When Sunny didn't answer or move, Drew glanced up. She was not paying attention to his words. She was looking at his knee.

"I want to check your knee."

Drew glared at Sunny until she met his stare. After a moment, he asked with quiet disdain, "Who do you think you are?"

Her heart in her eyes, Sunny looked at him with compassion and love. She could answer his question in many different ways, but she chose the easy answer—

the one he might listen to. "I'm a nurse. Remember? . . . I was there. I understand."

"Don't you *ever* patronize me," he growled.

"Patronize you? Is that what you think this is all about?" Sunny glanced away as memories filled her mind. "Don't you know that I cared? Couldn't you feel that? I cared more than I should have. Something happened to me. Something that has never happened before or since. No other person has ever stuck in my memory as you have. I've always wondered why your image was always superimposed over any other. . . ."

Sunny couldn't stop the memories or the words that poured out. "Certainly you remember that I stayed with you that first night. I stayed because I cared. Then I came up after my shift the next day, and the nurse said you refused to see me." She glanced away, remembering the frustration of being turned away. "Then bang, there you were the day you got hit in that intersection. I couldn't believe it was you. I couldn't believe Mike was your brother. And now I have no idea what I thought I saw in you. You're an angry, arrogant . . ."

"Boar. Isn't that the word you want?"

"That's one possibility. There are others I could use."

Drew grasped for control. "I don't need your help, but thanks for the ice. Be careful going down the stairs."

As if the last few moments had never transpired between them, Sunny gave Drew the special smile she saved for her most recalcitrant patients. When she had his attention, she asked, "Why don't you invite me to sit down?"

Drew shook his head.

Relief whistled through him as he watched Sunny turn around on her crutches. He wanted to call out that he needed the ice bag, but he'd do without rather than face her again. Drew listened for the door to open and close. Instead he saw her enter the bathroom. A moment later, she returned carrying a towel in one hand. Once again she stood over him. He'd never felt so vulnerable in his life, and somehow he thought she realized it.

Sunny sat down on an ottoman that matched the other chair in the sitting area, leaning her crutches against the wall. She was so close, she could reach out and touch him. She felt the heat radiating from his body, but she ignored the signals her own body urged her to act on.

"Does this usually happen when you ride, or did something unusual happen this morning to cause this kind of swelling?" When he didn't answer, she glanced up at him. His eyes were closed, but the muscle in his jaw jumped furiously. He was not as relaxed as he'd have her think.

Drew clenched his teeth. He was glad he'd taken the time to struggle into the shorts. What was he going to have to do to get this woman out of here—to get her out of his life? At the first touch, he thought she was finally placing the ice bag on his knee, but a second later, he knew it was not that impersonal.

His eyes flew open as he watched her hands examine his knee. Her touch was clinical, but in his heart it felt like the most sensual of caresses.

Sunny satisfied herself that his knee was extremely swollen and the surrounding tissue felt hot to her touch, but she didn't think any real damage had been done. If he stayed off it, kept the ice on it, and didn't abuse it on a regular basis, it would recover. She placed the towel across his knee and then settled the ice bag on it. Scooting back across the ottoman, she sat in the chair and propped up her feet.

Astonished, Drew watched her settle in as if it were the most natural place for her to be. He closed his eyes on the thought and took a deep breath. "I never took you for a person who would play games." Drew's voice was even, devoid of emotion.

Considering her answer, she searched his face just as she knew he was studying hers through half-closed eyelids. Sunny reached for her crutches and stood. She realized she'd pushed him far enough, but she did want the parting word.

With a calmness she didn't feel, Sunny looked at him. "You're right, I'm not a person who plays games. I know life is much too short for that, and I believe the human heart is too fragile to ever be played with unfairly."

After a moment she added softly, "Drew," pausing significantly until she knew she had his full attention. "As far as I'm concerned, this is not a game."

NINE

Outside Drew's bedroom door, Sunny slumped on her crutches and breathed deeply. She was emotionally winded. If she followed his lead, she'd quickly call a cab, wait for the taxi out on the porch, and send for her belongings at a later date. But she wouldn't give up.

Drew listened to the door close behind Sunny. His heart slammed in slow motion against his chest. He expelled the small amount of air he'd been able to inhale.

No, she wasn't playing games. He'd known it before he'd asked. Unquestionably she'd been serious, and her honesty, which was obviously an integral part of who she was, continued to unnerve him.

He let his head fall forward onto his chest. A frown marred his features. He didn't want to face her again. He didn't want to face himself either. He hardly recognized the person he'd become. She'd dealt with the harshness life could dish out, and yet she hadn't turned cynical as, he was forced to admit, he had.

None of this made any difference. Sunny would never be a part of his life. He had Jesse and he had Rico. For the past three years he'd needed no one else.

He pushed aside the voice that asked if he would feel the same in ten years. What then? Could he expect two adopted boys to fill the gaps in his life? He knew he couldn't—he wouldn't want them to. With his love, they'd both become healthy, whole individuals. If only he could say the same about himself.

A sudden noise shook him back to the present. Damn, if she'd fallen . . . he'd never forgive himself. Drew shot out of the chair, disregarding the ice bag as it fell, splattering condensation across the oak floor, disregarding the sharp pain shooting through his knee.

Sunny covered her ears as she watched her crutches clatter to the first floor. In the quiet house, the noise echoed as loud as a machine gun. Laughing, she wrapped her arms around her knee and rested her chin on it. When she heard Drew yank the door open, she raised her head again. Twisting around on the step, she looked up.

What he saw somehow returned a small portion of his long-forgotten sense of humor. Her soft laughter floated up the stairs and tore at his resolve.

The growing giggle died as Sunny met Drew's look in a heart-stopping embrace. It was as if every nuance of feeling that had ever occurred between them was relived in that moment. All the uncertainties, all the awareness, and all the need hovered in the space that separated them.

Consuela rushed in. "Thank heavens. I thought you'd fallen and broken something else." The housekeeper stood at the bottom of the staircase, wiping her hands on the apron that hung askew from her ample waist before she picked up the crutches.

With firm resolve, Drew shut the door. She didn't need him.

The bright morning sun glistened on the frosty path Drew slowly followed toward the barn. He needed to check on the stallion, but that wasn't his only objective this morning. His instincts were pushing him where his intellect was saying there was no need to go. Yet he knew better than to disregard them.

It would have been easier to ask Charlie to come to the house, but he wanted to see the new hired hand again. He had no proof, but the more he thought about it, the more certain Drew became that something about the man didn't add up.

The smell of horses and hay embraced him as he entered the barn and went to the stallion's stall. The horse whickered in recognition. Black Devil didn't look any worse for yesterday's wild ride.

Drew walked on toward the end of the barn, where he spotted Charlie, but his gaze drifted to the man who lounged against the wall. He could feel the man's insolence, tangible as the sneer that pulled his face every time Drew came near. This man did not match the perfect citizen portrayed on the computer printout on Drew's desk. Why was he working here? What did he want?

"How do you like working here, Farley? As well as South Dakota?" Drew asked.

"North Dakota."

Drew questioned him a moment longer, but Rob Farley didn't falter on any answer. He had the facts straight—his story was tight: Perhaps too tight?

Drew stood staring at him before he finally turned to Charlie. "I'd like to speak with you a moment."

When Drew was outside and certain the man could not overhear, he nodded back toward the barn and asked Charlie, "How's he working out?"

"Okay, although I don't feel too comfortable with him. That's why I usually keep pretty close tabs on him." Charlie took off his hat and scratched his head. "It's weird, Drew, but he kind of changes when you come around. Most of the guys put forth an extra effort whenever you come around, but with Rob, it's the opposite. I can't even explain it.''

Drew frowned. "Better consider letting him go, Charlie.''

"I have, but every time I think about it seriously, he comes through. It's as if he knows what I'm thinking and performs beyond his responsibility, or he reminds me about his sick mother, who receives most of his weekly check. And you know what a sucker I am for a line like that. But you're the boss.''

"Let it ride a little longer then. I'm going back to the house for a while. I want you to get him away from here. Ride fences. Check the east boundary. I need a couple of hours.''

"Ride fences?'' Charlie frowned. "I haven't done that in years. Besides, no one else is around the place right now. The others went into Albuquerque to pick up that new stud.''

"That's okay. I'll keep an eye on things.''

"What's going on, Drew?''

"I want to check out something while he's not around. Does he know as much about horses as he claims?''

"Sometimes I think he does, and then the next day I think he's lying. I called his references, and they checked out.''

Drew glanced at his watch. "Okay, I'll give you an hour.''

A few moments later, Drew opened the back door of the house, and his mouth tightened as he entered the kitchen. Sunny sat at the table reading the morning newspaper. Prince sat beside her with his paw resting on her thigh as she scratched behind his ears. The dog looked as if he were in seventh heaven. Drew clenched his jaw tighter. Removing his jacket, he determinedly reminded himself of his plan—be polite, a bit friendly, but no matter what, stay cool.

Sunny glanced over the top of the newspaper and watched Drew pull off his jacket. His shirt tightened across his torso. What she wouldn't do to get her hands on him . . . and his hands on her! The thought caused a flush of heat to travel the length of her body. She ducked her head behind the paper until she felt the color in her cheeks abate.

How could she look more beautiful every day? He turned away and poured himself a cup of coffee. Walking toward the table, he saw her eyebrows lift. "Want some coffee?"

"Yes, please." Sunny folded the newspaper inside out to the movie section and pushed it to the side of the table.

Drew placed the steaming mug of coffee in front of her.

"Thanks." Sunny sipped her coffee and watched as Drew sat down across the round oak table from her. She wanted to ask him about his knee, but she stopped herself. The pain he was experiencing was obvious from the way he favored his knee with each step and from the brackets of pain around his mouth.

Drew glanced at Sunny before looking out the large bay window, fixing his eyes, but not his mind, on the mountains. He wished he'd gone on to his office. He couldn't think of a thing to say, and he could feel her gaze on him like a warm caress.

Sunny cleared her throat. "Let's go see a movie tonight. You drive, I'll pay."

Drew frowned and opened his mouth to refuse.

Before he could interrupt, Sunny hurried on as she pushed the paper toward him and pointed to the ad for the movie she wanted to see. "It's received excellent reviews, and I need to get out. It's been almost six weeks." Drew looked up from the paper and met her eyes as she suddenly ran out of words.

With a smile tugging at the corner of his mouth, he asked, "Are you asking me for a date?"

Now, how was she supposed to answer that? The idea had taken shape as she'd read the morning paper. If she answered yes . . . But if she said no . . . She could see he was enjoying her quandary. She watched the smile lighten his stern features.

"What's your answer, Sunny?"

"What's *your* answer? Will you go out with me, Drew?" Sunny paused before she threw out an added challenge. "If you're up to it . . . we could even have dinner somewhere before. Anyplace you want. My treat."

"Can't. I've already got a date." If he hadn't been watching carefully, he might have missed the disappointment and hurt that flashed in her eyes before she lifted her chin a notch.

"How about tomorrow evening then?"

She never ceased to amaze him—nothing seemed to daunt her. Once again he felt outwitted, but he'd never let her know it.

"I don't know. I won't be home until . . . morning."

Unnerved, Sunny watched as Drew stood up and took his nearly full cup of coffee over to the sink and poured it out.

With a casualness he didn't feel, Drew walked to the kitchen door and turned back toward Sunny. "Tomorrow night? Why not?" The door swooshed shut behind him.

Another woman? Sunny had never considered the possibility. How unsophisticated and naive could she be? She felt like a little girl playing dress-up in the adult world, and everyone realized it was make-believe but her. Drew wouldn't be home until morning. He couldn't have been much more blunt than that.

Drew sat at his desk shaking his head. What a fool

he was. What had happened to his commitment to himself—his promise to keep his distance? Once again Sunny had outmaneuvered him, and he'd been unable to refuse her. A whole evening with her!

Dinner, a movie, and not just any movie. He'd heard a couple of the guys talking about it this last week. It was purported to be a great love story, and according to them, it had several R-rated scenes. But after a night with Sylvia, his cravings would be assuaged. He'd probably look at Sunny tomorrow and shrug his shoulders. It was certainly worth a try.

Damn! He'd forgotten the reason he'd sat down to talk to Sunny. Drew returned to the kitchen. "Could I borrow Prince for a couple of hours?"

Sunny mentally pulled herself back to the kitchen. In her mind, she'd been imagining Drew's body entwined with the body of another woman a beautiful woman who knew all the ways to please a man. When she finally responded, her voice sounded hollow. "Prince? Why? What's happening?"

Drew looked at Sunny, wondering why her voice sounded rather odd. "Nothing really." When he saw her chin go up a notch, Drew knew he might as well level with her right now. "I'm going to search the bunkhouse. I meant to do it yesterday. . . ." His voice trailed off.

Sunny suddenly recalled the events of yesterday in a different light. Most likely, he'd meant what he'd said. He wasn't interested, and he probably saw her as a pesky nuisance.

"I meant to ask you about Jesse. You never told me what happened that night you took Prince out to the bunkhouse. He wouldn't settle down for quite a while after you brought him back, and your telephone message didn't say much."

Drew joined Sunny at the table. Surprised, Sunny watched him call Prince to his side and pet the dog with great care. Leaning down, he spoke softly. She couldn't hear the words, but it was obvious he was trying to establish a rapport with the dog. Evidently he did believe in Prince's abilities. She wanted to gloat over the fact that he was asking to use Prince, but she knew this wasn't the time.

"I didn't give Prince a chance. He was agitated. It was all I could do to keep him by my side even on a leash. He obviously didn't like Farley. So I want to take him out to the bunkhouse while no one's around. I've talked to Jesse several times, and he sounds okay. Mike saw him and said he looked great, but I'm still concerned. I mentioned to him that there could have been marijuana in those brownies, but he didn't agree. Although all the facts say nothing is wrong, my instincts tell me something isn't what it seems."

"And as my dad always says, a good cop never ignores his instincts."

"Exactly. I learned that from him. Your father was one hell of a cop."

"He has a lot of respect for you."

Drew tried to keep his expression neutral but swallowed hard before he nodded, acknowledging the compliment. Sometimes he dealt with the changes in his life better than others. But sometimes, like right now, he rebelled against the drastic turn his life had taken.

Sunny absorbed the pain that flashed across his face as though it were her own. Knowing her silent understanding was all he would accept, she watched resignation settle across his features as he stared out the window.

After a moment she asked, "Do you want his leash?"

"Thanks. I'll get it if you'll tell me where it is."

When Drew returned, he held the heavy leather leash in one hand and a twisted and knotted towel in his other. Prince's demeanor changed immediately. Drew ruffled the dog's fur. "Good boy. Good dog. Let's go play."

Drew offered the towel to the dog. Prince took it greedily into his mouth and shook his head, growling. Drew continued talking to the dog as he stuffed a portion of the leash into his hip pocket and pulled on his leather jacket. A minute later, they stepped outside.

Sunny hopped over to the counter and poured herself another cup of coffee. Leaning against the counter, she looked out the bay window to watch. Drew and Prince were playing a vigorous game of fetch, but each time the dog retrieved the towel, Drew spent several moments loving him and talking to him before tossing the towel off in a different direction, sometimes even behind a bush, as if he didn't want him to find it.

Suddenly the play seemed to disappear before her eyes. She could see Drew was giving commands to Prince. She watched closely. He was rewarded with love each time, but the dog's enthusiasm had diminished. Drew snapped on the leash, and Prince immediately came to heel, acting as if he knew they had a job to do. The pair disappeared out of her sight.

Drew had ignored the prickling feel of Sunny's stare as he worked the dog, and he was relieved to be away from her scrutiny. He forced his mind to the business at hand. He'd never worked a dog before, but he'd give it his best shot.

When he'd talked with the training center this morning, the man had said it was a toss-up whether the search would be effective. Recalling the information he had received from the trainer who had worked with Prince, Drew checked Prince's reactions to certain commands. So far, the dog had responded as if he'd never missed a training session. The trainer thought the dog was probably right on target with the brownies. Damn! Why hadn't he believed Sunny?

Drew patted the dog and spoke gently. "Well, Prince, let's go see what you can do."

Prince walked beside him as if he were the most docile of family pets, but Drew remembered the dog Prince had become last Sunday night when he had faced Farley. The hair down the dog's back had literally stood on end. The question was why. He hoped he would have the answers shortly. Drew could see the change in the dog as they neared the bunkhouse. Prince was all business.

Drew opened the scarred oak door, and the pair stepped inside. He watched the dog lift his nose, moving his head from side to side catching scents before he dipped his head to the floor.

Drew unsnapped the leash. "Find it, Prince! Find it!"

Prince hurried around the room.

He stood in the middle of the living area and watched the dog, wondering if he knew what he was looking for. Drew wasn't even certain what they were after.

Prince ran toward the kitchen. The dog hesitated, his nose in the air. "Good boy. If you can smell anything besides burnt onions, it will be a miracle." Remembering to keep the dog motivated, he commanded, "Find it, Prince. Find it!"

Drew opened cupboards and peered inside. The dog stuck his nose in each of the cabinets as he quickly searched the room. He went back to one of the lower cupboards again. Drew pulled everything out, but there was nothing except an assortment of well-used pots and pans. Prince sniffed around the pans and stuck his head in the cabinet again, but he only wagged his tail.

"Okay, boy. I'll take your word on it. Let's keep moving."

Drew deliberately left Farley's bedroom until last.

He opened the door to the other rooms and gave each a quick glance, allowing Prince to roam at his own pace. The dog was in and out of every room within a minute. He wanted Prince to have a look, but he didn't want to invade the privacy of the men who had been in his employ for years—men whom he had no reason to doubt.

As he opened the door to Farley's room, he commanded Prince, "Find it, boy! Find it!"

He didn't know what he had expected, but he knew this wasn't it. Other than a mussed bed, there was no sign anyone lived here. Drew frowned as he turned around. He pulled open the top dresser drawer, then continued until he reached the fourth and final drawer. Nothing—absolutely nothing.

"What do you think, Prince?" When he turned back to look at the dog, he noticed the hair on the dog's back standing up.

Prince sniffed at the bed and circled it before he walked to the closet door and scratched.

"Good boy!" Drew opened the closet door. The contents were meager. A couple of changes of work clothes hung on hooks at the back of the closet. Pushed to one end of the closet were three hangers. Drew pulled them toward the center of the closet and reached up to pull the string, switching on the light bulb.

On the first hanger was a sport shirt with a pair of pleated pants that had the texture of linen. Nice, even classy. The next hanger revealed a black shirt. Drew touched it and instantly recognized the feel. He pulled the collar back. One hundred percent silk. Dry clean only. The black tag with embossed gold lettering heralded an exclusive men's shop in Santa Fe. In addition to recognizing the name, Drew realized the significance of it—the articles of clothing that were sold there were about 90 percent custom-tailored. The average man wouldn't think of going through the discreet double doors.

On the last hanger was a black leather blazer—buttersoft. Before Drew could follow the racing course his thoughts were taking, he tuned in to Prince's low, guttural growl.

"What is it, boy?" Prince was pawing at the end of the closet. Drew reached down and brought out a suitcase.

"Good dog! Good dog!" Recalling the trainer's instructions, he generously petted the dog.

It was a European satchel-style bag of the finest-quality leather. More puzzled with every second, Drew placed it on the bed. Brass fittings complemented the bag. A small combination lock was at one end. Good thing Farley had neglected to latch it. He'd hate to harm pretty boy's suitcase. Even as he unzipped it, the thought brought him up short: Rob Farley might dress the part of ranch hand, but what Drew was currently seeing screamed that the man was used to living life in the fast lane. Everything here spelled M-O-N-E-Y.

As soon as the case was opened, Prince was on the bed with his nose buried deep inside it. "Good boy. Find it."

Drew slowly lifted objects out of the suitcase one at a time. Prince lifted his head and sniffed at every item as it went past him, but each time his head went back into the case. Drew skipped over a few more articles of clothing as he heard Prince's paw hitting something that sounded like metal.

"What did you find, Prince? Good dog. Let me see what we have here. . . ." Prince continued to paw at the tobacco can that Drew held in his hands. "Okay, give me a chance to open it." Drew pulled up the lid.

"Nothing in here, boy. Looks like it's even been washed out." Drew lifted the can to his nose and sniffed. He could only smell the faint odor of stale tobacco—nothing more.

The dog stuck his head back in the suitcase and nosed around, but Prince quickly alerted back to the can. Obviously Prince smelled something he couldn't. He knew a dog's nose was ultrasensitive—many times more sensitive than his own.

Prince whined at Drew. "Good dog! I don't understand what you found, but you obviously think you're on to something."

Drew glanced at his watch. He'd learned years ago how to search a place and never leave a trace, and he returned the items without conscious thought.

Drew took one more look around the room before he pulled the leash from his hip pocket, fastening it to the dog's collar. "Good dog. Come on, Prince. We've got one more thing to search."

Drew circled the truck he knew belonged to Rob Farley. A four-wheel drive, two, maybe three years old—nothing spectacular, but certainly not economical either. Both doors were locked and the windows up. He loosened the tight leash he had on Prince and allowed the dog to sniff around the vehicle, but he alerted to nothing. Drew unfastened the leash.

"Okay, Prince, let's head for home." Drew watched the dog race ahead to the back door.

Startled by the noise of the door opening, Sunny sat up. She must have drifted off. Without thought, she swung her feet off the window seat, her heels hitting the floor with force. Pain exploded through her ankle and shot up her leg. She screamed.

The sound tore through Drew like a hot slicing knife. The door slammed shut behind him. His heart raced double time as fear gathered in his mind. Sunny was leaning over and holding her foot.

Drew yanked a chair out of the way and knelt at her feet, ignoring the wrenching pain in his knee.

"Sunny. What happened?" He slowly placed his hands on her shoulders. One hand reached up to touch the golden glow of her hair. It was soft, soft as silk, golden silk. . . . His voice was a hoarse whisper. "Sunny?"

Slowly she lifted her head. Drew watched tears trace down her pale cheeks. His hand came up to curve around her jaw, and his thumb swiped at a tear. Before he had that one wiped away, another followed in its path.

"Your ankle?"

She nodded.

Drew swiped at one last tear before scooting back so he could see her ankle. He could see her foot was swollen more than usual. He glanced up at her again and was glad to see a little color had returned to her cheeks.

Sunny wallowed in the concern she saw in his eyes. They had lost the frosty look of hard silver and were soft with warmth. "I must have dozed off, and when I heard you open the door, I swung my feet down without thinking. My foot landed like a dead weight, and it hurts like crazy."

"I can tell. Shall I call the doctor?"

Sunny shook her head. "Just give me a minute." She winced as Drew lifted her leg and carefully placed it on the window seat. He pulled out a chair to sit near her.

Her pain tore through his gut, chipping away at his resolve to keep her at arm's length. His heart urged him to enfold her in his arms.

Prince wiggled between them and whined. Sunny watched the pair as Drew absently petted the dog "What happened at the bunkhouse? Did Prince find anything?"

Drew recognized her tack—her need to think of anything but the pain. He frowned before answering. "I didn't find anything." He paused and rubbed the back of his neck. "On the other hand, I found more than I was looking for."

"Is this a riddle that I'm supposed to solve?"

"I wish someone could."

Mason succinctly answered each question his older brother fired at him.

"How tall?"

"Almost a foot." At his brother's frown, Mason added, "We knew the growth would be slow. Even though we're having a mild season, it's getting fairly cold at night."

"Any problems?"

Rob fidgeted in his chair as he listened to his older brothers. They were actually his cousins, but he rarely thought of them that way anymore. He'd gone to live with the Grangers at a very young age when his father had been killed. He was one of them now. They needed him.

Gus broke his gaze away from Mason to glance at Rob before shooting another question.

"Tell me about the lieutenant again. Day, time, the works."

"Hell, Gus. Oh, all right. It was Friday morning—midmorning, nine or ten, probably. I'd just poured the last of the coffee and doused the fire." At his brother's frown, he quickly added, "A small fire, very small, no smoke. It was real quiet that morning, no wind, just cool. I'd been dreaming about getting back home, back to Berty. Hell, both of you get to live indoors with a real bed. Me? I've got a sleeping bag on the cold ground."

"Want to trade places? Don't ever forget the only reason you're not here also is because of a small technicality." After a significant pause, Gus ordered, "When we've successfully accomplished our goal, then, and only then, can you go back to your life of luxury." He glared at both of them before adding, "Just don't ever forget whose brains have provided you with everything you have. Back to the *facts*, Mason."

"What I was trying to say was that it was real quiet. I heard this pounding noise—quite a while before I figured out it was a horse. I stayed out of sight. A minute later, the horse was practically flying by, within a hundred yards, a black one, and nobody but the lieutenant himself on his back."

Gus nodded quickly and glanced at the clock before looking back at Mason. "And?"

Mason continued. "He never glanced my way. Never saw the operation. Matter of fact, I don't think he was aware of anything. He and that horse never paused. They just shot across my vision and were gone within seconds."

The three men were silent for a moment before Gus glanced at the clock again. "Our time's about gone. Anything else?" he asked as he again noted Rob's fidgeting. "Robbie?"

"You know I hate it when you call me that."

"Something's eating at you. Out with it," Gus ordered.

"The next day, Saturday, the lieutenant came out to the barn. The other hands had gone into Albuquerque, so it was just Charlie and me. Anyway—" Rob took a deep breath "—he questioned me about the information on the application I'd filled out when Charlie hired me. It was obvious the lieutenant had read it carefully. He tried to trip me up, but it didn't work."

"What else?"

"Well, he talked to Charlie privately, and when the foreman came back to where I was working, he said we were going to ride fences, that we'd leave in about thirty minutes. Charlie didn't really say anything, but I could tell he wasn't happy about it.''

"Is this leading somewhere, Robbie?''

"I don't have any proof—just a feeling. I think someone went through my stuff while I was gone.'' Rob looked uncertainly from one brother to the other. "I think he searched my room while Charlie and I were gone.''

"When was this?''

"Yesterday.''

"Would he have found anything? Is anything missing?''

"No. Trust me,'' Rob entreated his brothers.

Gus finally nodded. "If this *is* true, it's obvious he's suspicious for some reason. Robbie, you be doubly careful this week, understand? Don't give *anyone any* reason to be suspicious about *anything*! And whatever you do, don't get fired. We're too close to the end for a slipup.

"Anyone that's ever had contact with him will tell you he was the best. Around here his name is lower than whale dung. Don't think he's forgotten a thing just because he retired.

"Don't either of you underestimate the lieutenant for even one minute. If it weren't for him, I'd never have seen the inside of this hole. He's about to learn that he can't infiltrate my organization for ten months and not pay.''

TEN

That evening Drew walked through the kitchen door, and the casserole she and Consuela had been enjoying suddenly tasted like so much dirt to Sunny.

A black tuxedo hugged his body, and he looked bigger than ever. Sunny's gaze traveled down his form; he was heart-stoppingly handsome. She wished she had the wherewithal to chain him to her bed, or better yet, to his bed. A pair of handcuffs would do fine with that heavy brass bed of his. She could keep him satisfied for a long time. She'd remove that tux piece by piece and thoroughly savor having him at her mercy. She'd take care of every need he had. There was no reason for him to go off to Santa Fe to visit some hussy. Her gaze slowly roved up his body to his dark eyes, which were now focused on her blushing face.

The doorbell interrupted Consuela's conversation with Drew. "I'll get that," the housekeeper announced.

Suddenly shy, Sunny glanced down at her plate.

The silence felt awkward, heavy. He'd seen the flush of desire in her eyes, but it wasn't his affair. Tonight he was going to solve his own problem. He turned when the kitchen door swung open. "Mom. I wasn't expecting you."

"I thought I'd surprise you. When I suggested coming out a couple of weeks ago, you rather put me off. Looks like you're out for a night on the town."

Drew watched as his mother introduced herself to Sunny. "My dear, Mike has told me such wonderful things about you. I'm glad I've finally gotten to meet you."

"Mrs. Williams," Sunny acknowledged, "it's nice to meet you."

"Call me Grace. Everyone does. This casserole smells delicious, Consuela. Is there any extra?"

As Consuela hurried to set another place, Grace looked at her son. "Drew, could you get my overnight bag out of the car?"

"Overnight bag?"

"Of course, dear. I've hardly seen you these last few weeks, and now I understand why."

When Drew returned, he said, "I put your bag in the blue room upstairs, Mom. Sunny's been using your rooms downstairs."

"That's perfectly all right. I hope you're not leaving."

"Sylvia and I are going to the symphony and dinner."

Sylvia. Sunny had a name now. She was probably lush and gorgeous and petite.

Grace glanced at Sunny and then at her son. "I'm surprised she has time for you what with that murder case she's taken on. She's really gotten a reputation for her style in the courtroom."

Sunny had been reading the daily paper regularly, and now she knew exactly who her competition was. A powerful trial lawyer. Beautiful, just as she suspected. Her shoulders sagged.

Drew's glance flashed to Sunny.

"I'll talk to you when you get home then, son."

"Don't wait up for me."

"You know what a night owl I am," Grace replied.

"He told *me* he wouldn't be home until morning," Sunny said. She hadn't realized she'd spoken her thoughts aloud until suddenly all eyes were focused on her. She felt like a third-grade tattletale.

Drew had heard the phrase "gnashing one's teeth." Now he knew exactly what it meant. Without glancing at either of the women again, he escaped through the back door.

"I'd hoped you'd stay the night, Drew."

Drew glanced at the beautiful woman who lounged across the room from him. He'd been the obvious envy of every man in the exclusive restaurant where they'd dined after attending the symphony. Without the program in his pocket, he'd be unable to tell anyone whether the symphony had played Mendelssohn or Mozart tonight. And dinner . . . It had cost a small fortune and tasted like sawdust.

He paced the living room of Sylvia's condo, a brandy snifter in his hand. He wanted to hurl the fragile crystal into the fireplace. Instead Drew placed it on the marble mantel with controlled force. If he had another sip, he'd not be competent to drive home until morning.

He turned and looked at the woman curled up in the corner of the couch. Her toes peeked out from the "something comfortable" she'd slipped into a few moments ago. Her jet black hair had been released from the pins that had held it in an artful pile all evening, and now it flowed over her breasts to her waist. He knew the scent and the texture of it. He wanted to carry her into the bedroom and lose himself in her, but every time he looked at her, he could see only Sunny's image. Sunny's strawberry blond hair, Sunny's freckles. Sunny—Sylvia. They were as opposite as two women could be. He silently cursed himself and yanked off the tie, stuffing it into his jacket pocket. He reached for the cummerbund, feeling annoyed with the confining clothes.

He respected and admired Sylvia, and she'd become a loyal friend. She had a brain like a steel trap, and they frequently enjoyed heated debates on every subject from international politics to a piece of artwork.

She was also an insatiable lover who boldly matched his own libido. But tonight . . . Tonight when they'd returned and he'd taken Sylvia in his arms, the usual explosion of passion had been absent. The kiss they'd shared had told him what he suspected—their relationship would never be the same again. And they'd both recognized she was not the one who had changed.

In a way, he supposed he could love Sylvia, but it wasn't the gut-wrenching, hell-bent captivation that lured him toward Sunny. Even if he was falling in love with Sunny . . . it wasn't in the cards for him to marry. Yet his growing feelings, and even the simple essence of Sunny's image, were preventing him from enjoying Sylvia tonight. And he could almost hate Sunny for it. What man in his right mind would consider a virgin over the passionate and ready woman sitting a few feet from him?

"Why don't you tell me about her?"

"Her?" Drew stared at Sylvia, but her eyes never wavered.

After a moment, Sylvia asked quietly, "How's your houseguest?"

Drew frowned and glared at her.

"Don't use that tough-cop look on me. It won't work."

"Quit using left-handed questions with me, Ms. Hard-Hitting Attorney. I've been reading about you in the newspaper."

"Don't try and change the subject, Drew. We've always been open and honest with each other."

"There's nothing to tell."

"And you wish there was?" When Drew didn't respond, Sylvia added, "It was thoughtful of you to let Sunny convalesce at the ranch."

"Humph."

"We've always said that if either of us fell in love, the other was free to go. Is that what this is all about?"

"And I told you I'd never let that happen."

"We don't always have control over our feelings."

Drew gulped the last of his coffee and walked to the kitchen. He felt like a caged animal. There was no escape anywhere. Drew knew he wasn't being fair to Sylvia, but what could he say? He needed to get out of here, but he didn't want to return home, where his heart beckoned him. He walked back into the living room and sat down again, closing his eyes.

"Do you want to talk about it? It might help."

"You've been a good friend, Sylvia, and if I don't talk to someone, she's going to drive me stark raving mad."

An hour later, Drew pulled into the driveway of his house, immediately glancing at the window of the room where Sunny slept. He turned off the headlights and then the motor. He stepped from the car and slammed the door with more than needed force, rubbing the back of his neck. He leaned against the front fender and stared at the window of her room. He ran his hands over his face, swearing softly.

His heart and mind continued the argument that had persisted since he'd left Sylvia's condo. It was a never-ending argument—one he couldn't harmonize between his driving need for Sunny and his logical mind, which shouted, *danger, no trespassing*. Thoughts of Sunny, of what it would be like to love her, had his body screaming for release. If he went to her, Drew knew he would never go with only his own needs in mind. He knew his heart would take over and a large portion of his craving would be to love her totally, beyond her wildest imaginings.

His mind reiterated the reasons and ramifications of what his heart was driving him to do.

Releasing a deep, shaky breath, he knew his heart was overriding the logic of his mind, crumbling the last of his defenses. He didn't want to continue to refuse the invitation Sunny's eyes offered every time she looked at him.

A light in Sunny's room flickered on, beckoning him like a beacon and dragging him away from the car. With settled resolve, Drew strode toward the house.

Sunny sat up in bed and turned on the bedside lamp. Had she heard a car door? Prince lifted his head, his ears pitched forward. The crystal clock on the bedside table read almost three o'clock. Moments later, she heard the click of his shoes on the oak floor. The sound stopped outside her door. Sunny held her breath as she watched the doorknob turn and the door open.

Electricity sizzled between the bed and the doorway.

Drew looked slightly disheveled. His tie and cummerbund were missing. The first three buttons of the shirt were undone. The jacket was clutched in one hand; the other still held on to the doorknob. Sunny wanted to rush into his arms, to rip the clothes from his body. She yearned to vanquish his self-control. She didn't move.

Drew clenched the doorknob to still the trembling in his hand. She wore the same gown he'd seen her wearing in the hospital—virginal white. The tiny buttons—enough buttons to drive a sane man crazy—would take him all night. The gown was pulled tightly across her breasts. His look met hers. Her sleepy smile destroyed the last of his control. Her innocence lured him. Drew's breath shuddered in his chest.

Prince stretched and walked toward Drew. He reached down and patted the dog. He stepped back, and Prince followed him through the doorway.

She listened to the soft command, "Stay," and watched Drew close the door in the dog's face. As she heard the distinct click of the lock, Sunny's breath caught and then quickened. Her hands curled over the satin comforter.

His focus on Sunny, Drew walked toward the bed, dropping his jacket on a nearby chair. He paused at the foot of the bed, watching her. Sunny's expression offered everything he could ever desire.

His voice, a sensuous caress across her heart, asked, "Are you sure, Sunny?"

The tip of her tongue moistened her bottom lip. "Positive, Drew." Her eyes followed the path of his hands as he reached for a tiny, black button on his pleated shirt. Her eyes widening, Sunny watched each button disappear. Drew slowly pulled the shirttail loose and unfastened the last button.

Sunny looked at the dark curls revealed by his actions. Her fingers kneaded the satin under her hands as her gaze locked with his. The faint stirrings that had been vague and unfamiliar just a few weeks ago budded and blossomed into full-blown cravings, spreading heat through her and settling low in her body. His smoldering gaze, the anticipation of his hands on her body, his mouth . . . his body . . . his obvious intentions, heated her body and tossed her into a swirling vortex of need—a need she knew only Drew could satisfy.

Never taking his gaze from Sunny, Drew pulled off his shoes and socks and reached for the waistband of his slacks.

Sunny's gaze raced to his hands as he reached for the zipper of the tuxedo pants. The jerky little breath she inhaled was audible in the silent room. Drew's hands shook as he lowered the zipper. The faint sound of the parting teeth of the zipper echoed, and a tiny shiver of anticipation raced up her spine.

Drew stepped out of the pants and flung them across the footboard. He lowered his gaze from Sunny's face. Her nipples jutted against the soft cotton fabric. Her hands twisted the comforter.

His black briefs bulged. Sunny felt her heart skip a beat before double time took over. Her lips parted. Her tongue traced her bottom lip. She lifted her gaze. Even as he approached the bed, she knew, without a doubt, this night would bring perfection to her dreams and satisfaction to her body.

His fingers flexed and then relaxed as he moved to the side of the bed. Drew dispensed with the covers, flipping them aside. He glanced at the cast, immediately disregarding all the implications. Settling on the edge of the bed, Drew gathered Sunny into his arms. His mouth, open and hungry, met hers without restraint.

When he pulled away from her, his uneven breath mingled with hers. Their gazes met and locked. It seemed as though this had been ordained by destiny from the beginning of time.

She'd waited for this moment for weeks—for a lifetime. Wild anticipation held her spellbound—awaiting Drew's next move. Pure hot desire poured through her veins, pooling in a deep, needful ache.

Drew traced the rounded neckline of her gown and reached for the first button, easing it through the tiny loop. He watched his hands, dark against her translucent skin, as he progressed to the next button. He felt no urge to hurry, only a desire to cherish each revelation. He could feel a tremble shift through her body.

Sunny reached up, settling her hands on his forearms. She felt his muscles tense under her hands before they began to tug and pull again as he unfastened each button. Why didn't he hurry?

Drew was in no rush, yet nothing could stop the inevitable, either. The release of each tiny button seemed to yield him more control. He reached for the next button, his knuckles brushing the inside swell of her breasts.

Sunny sucked in her breath.

He raised his eyes to hers. "Like that, do you?"

He'd barely touched her, and she felt hot and trembling. Her fingers tightened on his arms before returning to a caressing motion.

Drew continued his task, his hands trembling, until he'd unfastened the last button a few inches below her waistline. His hands slipped inside and curved around her waist, pulling the fabric farther apart. Her satiny skin was warm to his touch, almost hot. Drew heard her breath whistle lightly through her lips, a damp whisper against his neck. He lowered his head and grazed a kiss between her breasts. Her sweet scent surrounded him; waves of hot, urgent need warred with his fraying control.

His hair brushed her breasts. Sunny clung to his shoulders, wiggling a little, wanting to feel his hair tickle her breasts. She felt her breasts swell, her nipples tighten. Her nerve endings, almost raw with sensitivity, responded to Drew's every touch, creating an all-encompassing desire.

Drew raised his head and, with his fingertip, stroked the pulse point that hammered wildly in her throat. "Sunny?"

Her soft responding sound spoke volumes.

"You're beautiful . . . perfect." He traced a line from the beating pulse down . . . between her breasts . . . dipping into her navel. . . . Retracing his path, Drew pushed the gown farther aside, unveiling her breasts. His hands pushed the fabric down her arms, leaving her open to his quest.

His breath shuddered and he looked at Sunny's face. Her parted lips told him what he already knew: Desire—the counterpoint of his own—burned like an inferno. He reached up, threading his fingers into her soft golden hair. Placing a whisper-soft kiss below her ear, Drew stood.

He turned, and Sunny's heart stopped. He didn't dare stop now. She pulled her hands free of the gown and reached for him, but Drew ignored her invitation, stepping out of her grasp. She felt his look like a bold caress. He yanked off his shirt, dropping it on the floor.

Wanton yet innocent, Sunny stared at him. His chest and shoulders were broad and deeply corded with muscles. His hips were lean and tight. His hands rested on his hips, offering her the opportunity to look her fill. Male perfection. Her eyes roamed over his briefs, black and throbbing. She returned her gaze to Drew's face. His eyes, dark and proud, returned her look.

He reached for the pants he'd discarded. Sunny heard a faint sound and saw him place the small packet on the nightstand.

Standing at the side of the bed, he yanked the covers farther down and over the footboard. Sitting on the bed, Drew lowered Sunny onto the pillows and followed her down.

Her hands skimmed up his chest. Wanting to savor the feel of his skin but also wanting to explore every inch of his body, Sunny stopped only momentarily to tangle her fingers in the curls and explore the muscles. She relinquished the texture of his chest to thread her fingers through his hair, trying to capture his mouth, which was flicking tender, feather-light kisses across her eyes, around her mouth, and down her jawline. He stayed just out of reach of her searching mouth. He eluded her tug and looked at her.

"Are you with me, Sunny?"

"Yes."

"I've waited three long years for you. This fantasy . . . of you and me, together, has awakened me night after night. I want you with me every step of the way. I want our loving to be perfect for you . . . for both of us."

She felt his hands slide down to her hips before he lifted her, pulling the gown down. His callused hands, a raspy caress, slowly slid the length of her legs until he slipped the gown off over her feet, tossing it aside.

Her eyes drifted shut as she felt Drew's feather-light kisses across the arch of her foot, up her leg, to the inside of her thigh. Sunny felt the change. His lips were no longer whisper-soft. Drew now took tender, nibbling bites, up her thigh, around to the outside of her hip and across her waist, pausing to dip and swirl his tongue into the valley of her navel.

Naked and vulnerable, her senses tuned to his every touch, Sunny arched her hips, seeking Drew's possession to quench the blaze he ignited deep within her body. Her hands clutched at his shoulders.

At her touch, Drew slowly lifted his head and looked at her.

"Kiss me, Drew."

With a deep, responding groan, he answered her plea. Their bodies tangled in raw urgency. Hands, mouths, and tongues questioned, caressed, and devoured.

Sunny's body screamed for more.

Drew pulled back a bit, looking at her face flushed with desire. "Easy. Easy."

"No, I want it all!"

"And you'll have it all . . . in time." His voice only a hoarse whisper, he added, "But tonight let me set the pace."

Braced on his forearms, his mouth tugged on her

breast, sending a surge of exquisite torment swirling downward, dampening her femininity.

Sunny whimpered for more.

Drew gave in return.

Holding her hips, Drew eased himself into the hot, wet folds of her body. Encountering her body's natural refusal, he brushed a kiss across her eyes. "Look at me, Sunny."

Her hands tightened on his shoulders before sliding down to grip his arms. She opened her eyes. The man she loved hovered above her. Muscles corded his shoulders and arms. An artery in his neck stood out, throbbing. His eyes, dark and hooded, searched her face.

Sunny reached down and touched Drew where their bodies joined. Her fingers caught in the tangle of curls before seeking and circling his smooth, hardened flesh, which was partially buried in her own yielding flesh. She heard the sharp intake of his breath and saw the sheen of sweat on his tight, flushed body.

Sunny withdrew her hand and reached up to touch his lips. "I love you, Drew."

The scent of their bodies on her fingers and her pledge of love raced through his brain and burrowed deeply in his heart.

He had no words to speak, yet his body responded for what his heart could not utter. With a rough, infinite tenderness and a control he didn't know he possessed, Drew desired only to satisfy the passionate woman who writhed beneath him.

With the raw whisper of her name, "Sunny," he took not only the gift of her love but the yielding of her virginity to his passion.

Her heart bursting with love and her body greedy with longing, she felt Drew fill her. Sunny held his gaze. The pain was already a faint memory as the rhythmic ebb and flow of their driving desire hurled them into an untamed universe of their own. A creation where nothing existed but their hot, wet bodies begging and demanding until together they found completion in an explosion of pulsating pleasure.

Cradled in his arms, Sunny felt well loved and cherished, as if nothing could ever mar the new world their passion had created. Her fingers played their own unconscious game across his chest. She stroked his nipples, watching them bead, and felt his thighs tighten in response against her leg. She twisted the soft curls around her fingers. She loved the musky scent of their cooling bodies. Sunny lifted her gaze. "Drew?"

His callused hand, which rested on her hip, slid over the indention of her waist and slowed over the swell of her breast. His fingers grazed across her swollen lips. He touched his lips to her hair. "Sleep."

"Drew?"

He reached up and closed her eyelids with a soft motion before moving his hand down to caress her thigh. Moments later, he knew she slept deeply, but dawn crept into the corners of the room before he eased himself out of her embrace.

In no hurry, he began dressing. His gaze lingered on Sunny's sleeping form. Her cast—he'd forgotten about her broken ankle, about the reason she was here. In the light of day, Drew realized he'd forgotten a great deal more than that: He'd forgotten his promise to himself. He laid his hand on the cool plaster before he reached to touch her puffy toes with an absent caress. In an unconscious manner, he'd been aware of the cast during their loving, but the significance of it had not penetrated the sensual fog of his mind.

Drew rubbed his hand over his face, feeling the stubble of his beard and seeing the effects on Sunny's uncovered body. He shook his head in disbelief. He'd loved her with an intensity that still had him shaking. His mind had slipped into neutral, his heart had driven him. And their coupling . . . it had been perfect. She might never know just how beautiful their loving had been, but he did. Sunny's greedy response had touched him deeply . . . in the very gut of his soul as he'd never been touched before. And now he prayed to God that the memory would be enough to last him a lifetime, because he understood it could never happen again. The loving they'd shared could fast become an addiction he could never break.

What would happen now . . . in the days before she left? He pushed the question aside and gently pulled the comforter over her. He picked up her discarded nightgown, his grip wrinkling the cotton fabric. He placed it on the bed, and without a backward glance, Drew walked to the door. Letting Prince into the room, Drew quietly closed the door and trudged up the stairs.

He dropped his clothes beside the bed and collapsed facedown, burying his head under the pillow, the scent of Sunny's body still clinging to his own. Just before he fell into a deep sleep, Drew acknowledged just how cold and empty his bed felt.

ELEVEN

Sunlight, muted by the drapes, told Sunny the day had commenced without her. Turning over to glance at the clock, she saw her gown laid across the pillow. Hot, love-filled memories rushed through her body. The intimate beauty of the night brought a funny little catch to her throat and a soft smile to her lips.

At her movement, Prince stood and stretched before offering a sloppy kiss to her cheek.

"I'll let you out in a moment, Prince. I'm not moving until I remember every single detail of last night."

Drew . . . He'd said very little. Sunny could almost remember every word. But she'd needed no words—with his marauding hands, his conquering mouth, and his hard body, he'd left her with no doubt about his feelings. His tenderness—the time he'd taken making certain his fulfillment was secondary until her own was well spent.

Sunny smiled and sat up, reaching for the gown and pulling it over her head. He'd taken the time to unbutton every button. She'd never imagined love could be so beautiful, so perfect.

Remembering, she glanced at the bedside table. The

only remaining evidence of his "care" was a small edge of the wrapper. He'd thought of everything. . . . Whoa! Sunny sobered. He'd been with Sylvia just before coming to her—to her bed. He'd said he wasn't coming home until morning. Had he come directly from Sylvia's arms to . . .

She left the bed, and after a sponge bath that took more effort and time than usual, she slowly made her way toward the kitchen.

Sunny sat down opposite Drew at the kitchen table. Boldly they assessed each other across the space.

"Nice the two of you could join Consuela and me for a late breakfast." Grace smiled and then hurried on, "Rico's just finishing. I thought I might be the only one who'd overslept."

Sunny wondered what one said the morning after, especially with a mother and housekeeper looking on.

Drew. His hair was damp, and his face clean-shaven—obviously fresh from the shower. He looked at her, but other than his eyes looking a little wary, his face showed no expression.

Sunny looked different. A soft glow. Her lips. Drew closed his eyes against the hot images flooding his mind. The room was quiet, as if no one, not even Rico, wanted to break the silent communication between the pair.

"Is our date still on for tonight?"

"Date? How nice. Sylvia one night, Sunny the next."

Drew shot his mother a frown. "We're simply going to dinner and the movies, Mom. Sunny's been wanting to get out of the house for a while. We'd love to have you join us, right?"

Confused and a little surprised, Sunny stared at Drew and raised her chin a notch. She refused to give up her evening with him so easily. "Would we?"

"A woman who knows what she wants and goes

after it!'' Grace laughed softly. ''You remind me a lot of myself when I was your age.'' Grace glanced at Drew. ''You're outvoted, son. I'm leaving in a bit anyway. My bridge night.''

''Now that you're here, you might as well stay for a while. I've hardly seen you recently.''

''First you put me off and now you don't want me to leave.'' She winked at Sunny before adding, ''Thanks for the invitation, though, Drew.''

''Do you have those eggs ready, Consuela?'' Drew asked.

''Almost.''

Drew tried to tune out his mother's chatter, but her choice of topic made it impossible.

''Didn't I hear your car about three?'' Grace began with a shrewd smile that caused Sunny to blush. ''You must have gotten home a lot earlier than you expected. I don't think I heard you come upstairs right away, though.''

Consuela turned from the stove with Drew's plate, but he was already heading for the door. ''Forget the eggs. I'm out of here.''

''Me, too,'' Rico echoed.

Grace spoke as the two of them disappeared out the back. ''He seems a bit testy this morning. I hope I didn't say something wrong.'' Consuela and Grace both burst into giggles like young girls.

''I don't suppose you're going to renege on your breakfast, are you, Sunny?''

''Not me. I don't think I've ever been so hungry.''

Sunny missed the smug look that passed between Drew's mother and housekeeper.

That evening Sunny settled into the front seat of Drew's car and watched him as he walked around and slid into the driver's seat. As they picked up speed on the freeway, she wanted to reach across the console and rest her hand on his thigh, but she knew he wouldn't appreciate her advances.

It appeared they were at some kind of stalemate— one she didn't understand. Drew was the one who had initiated their loving last night. So why was he ignoring her? For now, silence seemed the only solution.

The traffic increased as they reached the outskirts of Santa Fe. Sunny wanted to ask where they were dining, but Drew seemed more than disinclined to break the silence. He seemed light-years away from the here and now.

She looked at his hands, which rested lightly on the steering wheel, remembering the feel of their caress across every inch of her body last night. A shiver raced through her at the thought.

She forced herself to look away, trying to focus on the surroundings. She always enjoyed the architecture and flavor of Santa Fe, but tonight it held no interest for her.

Even as his thoughts wandered and churned, Drew was aware of every breath Sunny took. Her gaze rarely slipped from his body, and it felt like a hot, bold caress.

Last night had forced him to search for his cobweb-covered dreams that had drowned in that arroyo. Did he dare dust them off and examine them carefully— inspect them for flaws? Dreams of a lifetime shared with a woman, of marriage, of children born of his own seed, of a love growing and aging like a fine wine . . . of sunshine in his soul. His dreams, he discovered, were not only covered with cobwebs but with years of cynicism.

Drew didn't recall anything except starting the car and leaving the driveway, yet they sat in the parking lot of the restaurant. He'd meant to consult Sunny about where she would like to eat, but his thoughts had driven courtesy from his mind. This was the best option anyway, considering their mode of dress. It had excellent food and was close to the theater. He rubbed at the tight muscles in his neck.

Sunny glanced at the filled parking lot. She'd heard of this place and knew it was difficult to get reservations days in advance. "Do we have reservations?"

"Uh, no. We won't need them." Moments later, Drew regretted he hadn't spoken to Carlos about a less secluded table. He had no desire to give Sunny the opportunity to initiate a conversation about what had taken place last night.

"Tell me, what did we do to deserve one of the best tables in the place?"

"The owner . . . I helped his son out once."

Before Sunny had time to respond, the waiter appeared. "Did you want to see a menu, or will it be the usual tonight, Drew?"

"Sunny?"

"Whatever you recommend will be fine."

Amiable as hell, he thought. For the first time this evening, Drew looked at Sunny carefully. Even after all these hours, she wore that well-loved look. He didn't know if he wanted to preen himself like a proud peacock fanning his plumage for his mate, or curse himself for surrendering to his desire.

A discreet cough from Carlos interrupted his self-examination. Ordering quickly, Drew returned to his thoughts. He was thinking like a hormone-driven fool. No. He was remembering Sunny had been a perfect lover. If he hadn't taken her innocence, he would believe she was experienced, very experienced. But the fact of the matter was that, even on their first—and only he reminded himself—time, they had met each other equally, passion for passion. Drew realized both of them had been fully satisfied. He felt heat tinge his face and hoped the candlelight hid his thoughts.

Sunny smiled, enjoying the flush that deepened the hue of his skin. But before she could discern his thoughts, Carlos placed wine and an assortment of appetizers on their table.

"Mm, this is delicious. I can certainly understand why this restaurant has the reputation it does." But when Drew seemed disinclined to contribute anything other than an unenthusiastic mumble or two, she gave up on conversation. The food that had been tasty a moment ago suddenly seemed tasteless.

It was obvious Drew was not experiencing the same excitement about their newfound relationship that she was. Questions flitted through Sunny's mind. She stopped eating and began pleating the napkin she held on her lap.

The silence that hovered between them was fraught with feelings. Feelings neither of them voiced.

Drew glanced up at Sunny, wondering why she'd suddenly stopped eating. She'd been enjoying her food, as always, he added to himself, but now God only knew what was going through her mind. Taking a drink from his wineglass, Drew decided he'd better choose a safe topic of conversation himself, before Sunny could dredge up the subject of last night.

"Why didn't you spend the night with Sylvia?"

Drew strangled on his wine, and if his napkin hadn't been handy, he knew he would have sprayed it across the table.

"If her picture does her justice, she's very beautiful," Sunny continued, ignoring his distress. "I saw her picture in the newspaper."

Wiping his mouth one last time, Drew feigned an aloofness he couldn't quite pull off and raised his eyebrows in question.

"Sir, I'll bring you a fresh napkin," the waiter interjected. Placing the hot plates of Mexican food in front of them, Carlos rushed away under Drew's glare. Returning just as quickly with another cloth, he placed it across Drew's lap with a flourish as he discreetly removed the wine-soaked one.

Sunny fondly watched the whole situation as she bit the corner off a *sopaipilla* and dribbled honey into the cavity of the warm bread. "Well?"

Having hoped she'd given up the question, it took Drew two attempts to swallow the bite of enchilada lodged around the lump in his throat. Her forthrightness scared the hell out of him. Buying time, he carefully placed his fork on the side of his plate and wiped his mouth with the fresh napkin. Taking a sip of wine, he set it aside and looked directly at Sunny. Somehow her tentative tone forced an honest answer from his depths.

"Damn it, Sunny." He swallowed hard, wishing he could lie to her, knowing he couldn't—not about this. "That's a question you shouldn't be asking me. All you need to know is that I didn't. Satisfied?"

"Now? No. Last night? Totally."

Her sensuous smile set flame to his smoldering passion. He felt her hand boldly touch his thigh. And to think he'd once thought of her as an angel. Overnight she'd become a practiced temptress.

As she returned to her dinner, Drew watched a frown form and deepen. He'd rarely seen her frown. "Now what is it?"

Sunny shook her head. "Never mind."

"Sunny." Her name a low caress, he reached across the table and took her hand, his thumb circling her palm. "Sunny?"

Shivers danced down her back, kindling a small fire in her body. "I feel . . . awkward, to say the least. You came from her arms . . . her bed . . . to me."

"It wasn't like that."

Sunny glanced up at him, not caring if the sheen of her tears showed, and whispered, "You obviously were planning to make love to someone."

Drew's eyes widened and darkened in understanding. "Did you want me to come unprepared?"

"No . . . I don't know." She withdrew her hand from his caress.

"You're obviously not on the pill."

"How do you know that?"

Drew leaned back in his chair, grasping for the right words. "I've been through your purse, and I didn't see any. There weren't any in your bathroom when I packed your things, either."

Sunny flushed. "Damn you, Drew. I know so little about you, and I feel like you know everything about me."

Drew rubbed the back of his neck. "This conversation isn't going anywhere. If you'll excuse me for a moment, I want to speak with the owner before we leave."

Sunny watched him walk away from the table. She needed to understand him. She wanted a commitment from him; she'd settle for a hint. Yet Drew offered her nothing. She was in limbo. Hopes raised—hopes dashed. Had he simply used her? No, she could never believe that.

Sunny felt as if Drew had given her a morsel of candy last night, and today she had a greedy appetite, but he'd locked her out. Now she could only stand outside the candy store, her nose pressed to the glass, looking in, lusting for another taste.

Drew returned to the table and, after a moment of strained silence, said, "I just want to say one thing. None of this really matters anyway—" he paused, taking a deep breath "—because, mark my word, Sunny, it won't happen again. Ever!"

Sunny sat in stunned silence as Drew returned to his meal with enthusiasm. It was as if he had waved a red flag in front of her. Resolve returned in force. Sunny pushed her plate away and leaned on the table with her arms folded.

"I've heard that line before, haven't I? And I proved you wrong. Last night to be exact." When Drew had the decency to flush under her stare, she continued. "I may be inexperienced, but that wasn't sex last night. That was an . . . an expression of love. It was more than beautiful. And as I've said before, it will happen again—ASAP."

"ASAP?"

"Yes. As soon as possible. Preferably tonight."

Shocked, Drew watched Sunny scoot back in her chair and pull the plate toward her. She ate until every bite was gone, readily accepting dessert and coffee when Carlos offered.

"I think you could almost eat more than me," Drew muttered.

"Probably," she returned.

"How do you stay so slender?"

"Jogging. I've been doing calisthenics each day since I can't jog. But I'll be back to it real soon."

"Mike says you're almost obsessive when it comes to jogging."

"Probably true. Ten to twelve miles a week is all I've had time for recently. It will take a while to build up to that again with this ankle."

"Isn't there a chance you won't be able to take up jogging again, or at least not right away?"

When she refused to look at him or answer, Drew spoke gently. "I know it was a bad break. Just what is the long-term prognosis?"

"I can't consider the possibility of not being able to jog."

Denial. Drew nodded in understanding. He'd recognize it anywhere. "What exactly did the doctor say?" When she didn't answer, he prodded, "Sunny?"

"Just that with this type of fracture, it could take a

while, that I might not be able to jog like before." She glanced away from the understanding in Drew's eyes. Taking herself in hand, Sunny declared, "But it will be fine, Drew. I'll jog again . . . and soon."

"Are you forgetting who you're talking to? Sometimes determination is simply not enough."

Before Sunny could respond, Drew stood and reached for his wallet as Carlos placed the bill on their table.

"No, my treat. Remember?" She pulled a charge card out of her pocket and waved it at Carlos.

"Never. I've never let a woman pay for my meal."

"You know, there's a name for a man like you."

"Don't even think of uttering it."

"Then let me pay. You can buy the popcorn at the movies. This was my invitation."

He suddenly relaxed and laughed.

She fell in love all over again.

"You're going to eat popcorn after all that?"

"Probably a candy bar, too. If you'll pay, of course."

Drew grabbed her credit card and pocketed it before she could make a scene. But on the way to the car, he handed it back to her. "I don't see how you could have any credit left to charge dinner after that shopping spree that was spread from one end of your room to the other. Just what did you have in mind when you purchased all that satin and silk?"

"Seduction?" she asked with a secret smile.

"Yeah," Drew growled.

Sunny sat, riveted by the romantic comedy that played out on the screen before them. The credits rolled, but the popcorn was untouched and the unopened candy bar was almost melted from her tight grip.

Outside the theater, Drew stopped her. "If you want to wait here, I'll get the car and save you the walk."

"I'd enjoy the walk if you don't mind my slow pace."

"Fine by me."

The chilly night air did not ease the desire that stirred her body. The movie had been a wonderful story, but the love scenes had been almost graphic, causing her to fidget, returning her thoughts to the ecstacy she'd found in Drew's arms last night. She took a deep breath and stopped in the middle of the brick walkway. "We could rent a motel room."

Drew stopped dead in his tracks and turned toward her, gripping her arms. "My God, Sunny. What do you want?"

"You." Silence spread between them. Sunny dipped her head. "I'm sorry. I don't know what possessed me to suggest such a thing."

Drew continued to stare at her. Wanting so much. Reminding himself he had no choice but to deny them both.

Sunny whispered, "Please don't ever remind me of what I just suggested."

Drew's responding chuckle ended her self-consciousness.

"And don't laugh at me, ever."

He sobered immediately. "Never. I could never laugh at you." He reached out. The pad of his thumb traced the fullness of her bottom lip, dipping in to touch the edge of her teeth.

Sunny's tongue savored the rough texture of his thumb. A shiver ran the length of her spine.

"Let's get you to the car before you freeze."

"I'm not cold."

Their gazes locked.

"I'm well aware of that."

The return trip to the ranch was made in moody silence; Sunny's thoughts rushed one way and then the other. She was certain of her love for this man, but his feelings for her . . . She thought he might not yet realize he cared as much as she did. She had doubts one moment, and in the next she knew last night could not have been so perfect without his love.

Drew could not decide whether to hurry home and get her off his hands or to measure the miles, enjoying her nearness and the scent of her body filling his car.

As he pulled into the driveway, Drew's desire for the woman beside him ebbed as he glanced at the house. "There must be a problem. It's late, and most of the lights are on." Drew parked quickly and helped Sunny from the car. As he shut the car door, the housekeeper stepped out on the porch.

Sunny managed the loose gravel slowly, and she could feel Drew's impatience. "Go ahead. I know you're worried."

"It's okay. Another minute won't matter."

"Consuela? What's wrong?"

"Well, I don't really know. Did you two have a nice time?"

"Did you stay up to check on us or is there a message for me?"

"A message . . . from Jesse. He sounded upset. He called about an hour ago."

"I'll call him," Drew called over his shoulder.

Consuela closed the front door and watched Sunny watch Drew disappear down the hall to his den. "Would you like some hot chocolate, Sunny?"

Sunny frowned. The evening wasn't ending as she'd hoped. Matter of fact, she'd been counting on it not ending until morning. Seeing no options, she followed Consuela into the kitchen.

Before the milk had warmed, Drew entered the kitchen. "I'm going to Albuquerque."

"What's wrong?" Consuela asked.

"I don't really know." Drew flicked a glance at Sunny before he said, "Don't wait up for me."

Hopes dashed, Sunny nursed her cocoa. She didn't feel like chatting with Consuela, but she didn't want to go to her room either.

An hour and a half later, Drew sat across from Jesse in an all-night coffee shop. Jesse had finished off a plate of nachos with a large soda, and now he fidgeted with his coffee cup, sloshing the brown liquid onto the saucer.

"Come on, Jesse, talk to me. What's happening?"

"I think you were right. Those brownies . . . Ever since then, I've been fighting the desire to use again. Fighting it like I haven't had to since my days in treatment. I called John, but he's out of town, and I guess I was a little desperate and called you."

John was Jesse's Narcotics Anonymous sponsor, and Drew was grateful to him. The man had really helped his son through some rough times. Jesse wasn't nearly as dependent on the organization as he once was, but Drew knew he still kept in close contact with his sponsor.

"Hope I didn't ruin your date."

"It wasn't really a date. Just Sunny. She wanted to get out of the house."

"Consuela called it a date."

"Consuela would. But let's talk about you."

"I'm okay now. Seeing you has helped. I'll make it. One day at a time."

"I know you will, Jesse. I'm proud of you."

Sunny tossed and turned. She'd left the light on, waiting. Another hour passed. When she finally heard Drew's car, her heart skipped a beat, then accelerated. Hearing the front door close, she held her breath, listening.

Drew glanced at Sunny's door. He noted the obvious invitation: Her light was on. He never broke stride as he went up the stairs to his own room and locked the door behind him.

Jesse's phone call had been an easy way to end the evening. He hadn't known if he would have had the strength to leave Sunny, but Consuela's message had put a damper on his rising desire.

He stripped and climbed into bed. Lying on his back with his hands behind his head, Drew pondered the corner he'd painted himself into. There was only a week until it was time to get her cast off, until she left. He'd be damned if he'd allow himself to get into a situation that could lead to anything again—no matter how much he wanted it.

TWELVE

Sunny waved out the kitchen window at Rico when he glanced her way. As she'd promised, she was watching Rico and Prince playing a wild game of Frisbee. Prince was going to miss Rico when they left. It seemed as if this last week had flown by, leaving only a week until she could have her cast removed.

Sunny frowned as Prince's demeanor changed instantly. A man walked toward the pair, but she relaxed when she saw Rico wave to the man as if he knew him. He must be one of the ranch hands, Sunny decided. Prince was just being protective of Rico. But still, she didn't like the dog's reaction and she moved toward the back porch.

"Hi, Rob. What are you doing?" Rico asked.

"Not much. Just out looking around, walking off my dinner. Hey! Nice dog you got there, Rico, but he doesn't seem too friendly."

"Yeah, he's really smart. I wonder why he's growling at you that way, Rob."

"Maybe he just doesn't like strangers. Some dogs are like that."

"Prince used to work for the police, looking for

drugs and chasing the bad guys just like my dad used to do."

"Oh, really? Your dad used to chase bad guys?"

"Yeah. He helped put a lot of them in prison, where they belong."

"How did you get the dog, Rico? I haven't seen him around until recently."

"He belongs to Sunny." Rico glanced toward the window, and Rob followed his gaze, but Sunny wasn't there. Rico frowned. "That's the lady who's staying with us till she gets her cast off. She couldn't stay by herself. I wonder why Prince is acting so weird. I've never heard him growl before."

"Do you know how she got the dog?"

"Look, Rob, his hair is standing straight up on his back. Feel it."

Rob took a step toward Prince, then backed away. "I don't think I better. He looks like he'd like to bite me."

"He only bites bad guys, Dad said." Rico cocked his head to one side and asked, "Are you a bad guy, Rob?"

"Are you kidding? Your dad wouldn't let me work here if I was a bad guy, now would he?"

"No, he sure wouldn't."

"So, Rico, why doesn't Prince work for the police anymore? Wasn't he any good?"

"Oh, no. He's good. Really good. Prince knows everything, but he gets sick or something, Sunny said. So now he's her dog, but I'm taking care of him while he's here."

"Why don't you show me just what he can do?"

"I don't know how to make him do very many tricks. Well, some of them aren't really tricks."

"Oh, I bet you can really make him do some neat things."

"Well, yeah."

Sunny had heard the end of the conversation as she stepped out on the back porch, but that didn't concern her as much as Prince's obvious mistrust of the man. "Rico?"

"Hi, Sunny. This is Rob. He likes your dog, but Prince is acting weird with him."

Sunny gave a stiff nod in response to the introduction. She could feel the man's eyes devouring her. She was used to men looking, but this man was giving her an odd feeling, and it certainly wasn't positive.

"Come on out, Sunny."

"Thanks, Rico, but I think you better come in."

"Ah, Sunny."

"I'm getting tired. I thought we might finish that adventure book before dinner. I think we have just enough time."

"All right. See you around, Rob."

When Rico got to the porch, she called to Prince. The dog was still watching the man disappear across the yard. "Who is he?"

"That's Rob. I don't know his last name. He works for my dad with the horses. He's always really nice to me."

With an uneasy feeling, Sunny watched the man until he disappeared down the path toward the barn.

Drew had gone to Albuquerque to check on Jesse again. Sunny had waited up for him last night, deciding she needed to talk to him since she couldn't throw off the uneasy feeling about Prince's reaction to Rob. But Drew had called and said he was spending the night at Mike's and wouldn't be home until sometime today.

She'd lain awake wrestling with her thoughts until almost dawn and had finally fallen into a deep, dreamless sleep. Her thoughts had not been on the dog but on her relationship with Drew. She'd only be here a few more days, and she couldn't wait to get rid of the cast, but Sunny feared once she'd left, her chances would be slim or even nonexistent of winning Drew's trust and his love.

Drew had been unfailingly polite during the week since they'd made love, but he'd kept his distance as he'd vowed to do in the restaurant. He didn't touch her at all, but at times, when she caught him staring at her, it felt like the hot flick of his tongue on her skin. She knew with a gut feeling he was interested—she'd bet more than interested—and she continued to fall back on the assumption that he could not have made love with her the way he had without a deep feeling. She was betting on it being love.

They had talked and argued about everything—well, not everything, nothing terribly personal, but their likes and dislikes, music, books. Sunny had been pleased how well their interests had meshed.

She'd given him the physical space he seemed to demand, but her time was running out, and during the sleepless night, she had come to a decision and formed a plan of sorts.

She'd slept the morning away, and when she'd gotten up, Consuela had informed her she would be gone until quite late in the evening, but that Drew would keep Sunny company. A few hours ago Drew had left to drive Rico to a neighbor's ranch for his best friend's birthday party. Sunny had escaped to her room for the afternoon on the pretense of finishing a novel she'd been reading, but really it was simply to wash her hair and decide what to wear. The afternoon had dragged by.

The sun had set and the house was absolutely quiet as Sunny walked down the hallway and stood in the living room doorway, watching Drew. He knelt in front of the fireplace, placing kindling and then small logs on the grate. She closed her eyes, remembering the feel of his hands, of his body, of his love.

Drew had been aware of her from the moment she'd come into the doorway. He'd felt her hot gaze traveling his body. He spoke as he struck the match to light the fire. "With that wind blowing, I thought it might get cold."

Sunny walked into the room, and he turned around, giving her a quick once-over. Not knowing exactly what to do and suddenly feeling awkward under his gaze, she spoke. "I'll be leaving in a few days. I appreciate all your help, Drew. Letting me stay here. Everything." Even to herself she sounded like some frigid fool.

Drew raised his eyebrows at her little speech. "You're welcome." He was surprised at her unusual awkwardness. She nearly always appeared to have total confidence, but a closer look at her face revealed she was truly uncomfortable. Still, she looked enticing in the soft sweater clinging to her breasts, which rose and fell quickly under his gaze. But then, she looked good in a Garfield nightshirt, too.

"Come on in and sit down. Enjoy the fire. Where's Prince?"

"I just let him out."

"I guess Consuela left us to fend for ourselves this evening." There had always been someone in the house besides the two of them, but not tonight. If it hadn't been Rico's best friend's birthday party, Drew wouldn't have let him go. But he couldn't hide behind Rico or anyone else. He'd managed fairly well to keep his distance during the past week. But tonight . . .

Drew quickly buried the thought. "I put the casserole in the oven a while ago. It should be almost ready to eat."

"Smells good."

"We might as well eat in here where we can enjoy the fire. Would you like a glass of wine with dinner or are you still taking the pain pills?"

"Wine sounds wonderful."

Drew realized they were dancing around each other like two boxers in the ring, wondering who would make the first move, who would make the first mistake.

Standing in the kitchen, he cursed himself. Why had he suggested they eat by the fire? How intimate. Seduction served on a platter. The only thing missing was soft, romantic music, but he knew they could create their own in perfect harmony. He knew they needed nothing but each other. The chemistry between them was evident no matter where they were or what they were doing. His body was like a combustible material waiting for the torch of her touch.

With a laden tray in his hands, it was Drew's turn to stand in the doorway to the living room and look at Sunny. Wary of himself, of his lack of control, Drew entered the room slowly.

Sunny heard him and glanced back from her place on the sofa.

"Want to sit on the floor in front of the fire?" He cursed under his breath.

Sunny smiled. He seemed to be thinking along the same lines she was. Maybe he had arranged the evening so they could be alone.

Drew put the tray down on an end table and watched her as she scooted off the cushion and sat on the floor. She leaned against the sofa and smiled up at him.

He poured the wine before sitting down beside her, pulling the tray between them like a defensive shield.

They quickly ran out of chitchat, finishing their dinner in silence. Only the howling wind and the sound of the logs settling echoed in the room.

Drew reached for the bottle of wine and refilled their glasses. "There's dessert if you want it."

"No, thanks, this was delicious. I hate to think of eating my own cooking after Consuela's."

"She thinks you're the greatest, too, and she never misses an opportunity to tell me so."

"And you resent that."

"Hell, yes!" He shook his head. "I'm sorry, Sunny."

Both of them lapsed into silence again as the room quickly darkened except for the light of the fire.

He wanted to touch her, needed to touch her, but he'd be damned if he would. His body felt like an archery bow strung too tight. If the tension didn't ease . . .

Drew grabbed the tray, none too gently, and set it aside. Turning back toward Sunny, he pulled her into his arms. Just before his mouth opened on hers, he spoke in a harsh, angry tone. "Damn you, Sunny."

With the first stroke of his tongue, she became soft, pliant, and giving. Her surrender taunted him, fueling his growing confusion. He wanted her out of his house. He wanted her out of his life. He wanted her beneath him. He wanted her for a lifetime. He hated his inability to cut her out of his thoughts.

His escalating desire ended his battle with himself, and his mouth gentled, coaxing a deep moan of pleasure from Sunny. Pulling away, he yanked off her sweater, revealing a soft, creamy-colored camisole. His hands rushed to slide over the slippery texture of the silk, her nipples budding under his caress. Knowing the perfect pleasure that could be his, hot, mindless need built quickly. "Sunny, you feel so good, so perfect. Your skin is like satin."

Sunny arched her body, desiring more of his touch. Wanting the feel of his skin against her body, she fumbled with the buttons on his shirt. Her hands pushed the material aside, and Drew, responding to her need, released her momentarily to help remove the shirt. Her hands raced across his nipples before sliding down the slope of his chest to his belt buckle.

Drew's mouth covered hers again, and his tongue pronounced his desire as he reached to help her. He paused to give her the space to unfasten the zipper, and she slid her hand inside.

"Touch me," he asked greedily. He pulled back a bit, wanting to see her face as she explored his body. The firelight flickered across her features. The flush of desire enhanced her beauty. He whispered, "Sunny."

Her body ached for fulfillment, and her voice was but a thread of a whisper. "I love you, Drew. Marry me."

Drew jerked away from her embrace and rolled to his feet. A half laugh, half groan came from somewhere deep within him . . . somewhere where the essence of his hopes and feelings resided . . . took on new meaning, expanded, and exploded, disintegrating into despair and heart-wrenching pain.

"Are you out of your mind?" Had her words been a question or a command? he wondered.

The heat of desire fled under his words, and Sunny suddenly felt young and naive. She sat up, realizing he was in a much further state of undress than she was, yet feeling totally naked. With his fists clenched on his hips, he towered over her, staring at her. She glanced down at his jeans, unzipped and slung low, very low, on his body.

She glanced away and reached for her sweater. Sunny hugged it to her body as if to protect herself from his angry, flashing eyes, which were turned on her as if she'd said something devastating, as if she'd told him he had an incurable disease.

With hands that trembled, she slowly pulled on the sweater. Tears pooled in her eyes. She refused to let them fall. She refused to let him see her anguish. How could he be so unfeeling? How could she have been so stupid?

"No, Sunny, I won't marry you."

As if beseeching him to stop his refusal, she looked up at him. His words were merciless, but she needed reasons for his unconditional rejection. "Why? Don't you love me?"

His heart betrayed his will. "Hell, yes. I love you!" God, but she had nerve, he thought. How had she dragged that fact from him? He hadn't really admitted it to himself. "But I'm not going to marry anyone . . . ever."

"How can you know that?"

"Easy. It was a decision I made years ago."

He was holding himself in strict control, and she hated that, especially when she was falling apart, emotionally naked for his viewing. Sunny was surprised at her ability to follow his words. "I assume the reason has something to do with your accident?"

"You're damned right!"

Ah, she thought, at least he showed some emotion over that. "Do you know that I love you?"

"Yes." His tone was almost a monotone. Drew's clipped but polite answer grated on her frayed nerves. Her mind wildly searched for a way past his composure. She wasn't going to give up without a fight. She'd never imagined he would turn her down so flatly, so unemotionally.

"And you said you loved me." When he didn't respond, she asked, "Could you explain what your accident has to do with marriage? It certainly didn't render you . . ." She was blushing, and she could see he was almost enjoying it.

"Impotent? Is that the word you're looking for?"

Sunny pushed herself up and onto the sofa. "Why are you avoiding my question?"

"I'm not. The answer should be obvious to you."

"It isn't."

"Damn it, Sunny. I'm a cripple; anyone can see that."

"Does that mean you can't support a wife? Is that why? Well, I can support myself quite adequately. What can't you do? Tell me!"

"Don't be obtuse, Sunny."

"So, because occasionally you limp slightly, because you can't go backpacking with Rico, or in other words, because you're not as perfect as you once were . . ." Sunny watched him flinch but asked, "Is that what this is about? I realize there are many activities you can't participate in now—your job being the biggest factor. But please tell me, how does that involve your heart and your ability to love?"

When he turned away from her gaze, Sunny reached for her crutches and stood up. Walking over to where he stood staring into the fire, Sunny stood beside him, looking at his stoic profile. A muscle jerked wildly in his jaw, but otherwise he acted as though they were discussing the weather.

He'd written the book on self-control, and Sunny yearned to drive him beyond it. Her voice quavered, and the pooling tears slipped slowly down her cheeks. "So this really isn't about the love we feel—the love that could grow into something beautiful between us. This is about you—without regard for me. I really don't enter into this at all, do I?" When he didn't respond, Sunny reached up and touched his cheek where the muscle jumped.

Anger ended her tears and hardened her voice, her resolve. "I can't believe it. You have everything—a beautiful home, a family who loves and respects you, and your health." When she saw him flinch, she added, "Yes, your health. But you're afraid of living, of giving of yourself, of committing yourself to a woman . . . to me . . . because your body isn't perfect?

"You think of yourself as a cripple? Well, let me tell you something. I agree." He turned to look at her, his eyes flinty hard, but she didn't flinch from his gaze. "You *are* a cripple, Drew, but only in your mind."

He turned to watch her ungainly exit. He wanted to call her back, to take her in his arms, to bring their loving to climax. The moment she was out of the room, Drew expelled the breath he'd been holding. He picked up Sunny's wineglass and hurled it at the fireplace. He missed, hitting the mantel. He picked up the other glass and threw it into the fire. Pain tore through him like an exploding bullet. He hated himself and what he'd become. If only he could hate her!

Sunny heard glass shattering, but she didn't pause in her escape. Sitting on the edge of the chair in her bedroom, she wrapped her arms around herself. The slam of the front door reverberated throughout the house. Hearing the engine of a car, she went to the window. The headlights from the Bronco flashed across her body. A moment later, Prince scratched at her door.

"Well, Prince. If I can find a way, any way, I'm going home, tonight. You'll have to stay here for a couple more weeks until I can exercise you myself."

Sunny banked every emotion and busied herself, awkwardly dragging her suitcase from the closet, placing it on the chair. She quickly filled it with her clothing. Taking her oversize purse into the bathroom, she swept the articles off the counter and into the bag, not caring if anything spilled or broke.

She reached for pen and paper and wrote a note to Consuela and then one to Rico, asking him to take care of Prince until she could return to get the dog. The one to Drew took no time at all. What could she say? Zipping the suitcase closed, she walked to the kitchen and dialed the bunkhouse, asking for Charlie. She'd only met him once, but she hoped he'd do a favor for her.

"Charlie? This is Sunny. I need to get to Albuquerque, tonight. I hate to impose, but could you take me?

"Yes, it's important I leave tonight. As soon as possible. No, Drew's not here. Thanks, Charlie. I'll be waiting."

Two hours later, the ranch foreman pulled up in the driveway of her house. The calm she'd forced herself into almost shattered at the sight of her childhood home. A home where she'd felt secure and loved. A home where life had been good. A home where she knew no failure. But tonight her world had shattered. And yes, she felt like a failure tonight. Somehow, something had gone grossly awry.

Reassuring Charlie, she closed the door behind him. The house was cold—the kind of cold that comes from being unoccupied. The same kind of cold that filled her heart. Sunny dropped her purse beside the suitcase and slid to the floor, her back against the cold front door.

Dry, choking sobs tore through her as she huddled in a heap.

Drew sat slumped over his early morning coffee, not wanting the breakfast Consuela was preparing.

"What happened here last night?" Consuela asked.

"What are you talking about?" She'd probably seen the mess in the living room.

"Sunny."

Her name was enough to return the steel to his backbone, and he sat up straight and looked at his housekeeper. "It's really none of your business, Consuela."

"When a girl, who happens to have become my friend, packs up and leaves in the middle of the night, I'd say it's my business. If she wanted to go home so badly, why didn't you take her, instead of making Charlie do it?"

Spilling his coffee, Drew stood, bracing himself on the table. "What are you talking about?"

"What am I talking about?" She looked at Drew.

"You really don't know, do you? I thought you were going to be here last night."

"I was here . . . but I left."

"Charlie drove her to Albuquerque. Why do you think she left so quickly? She didn't really say in the letter."

"Let me see the letter."

"Didn't you get one?"

"Not that I know of."

"Did you look for one?"

"Damn it, Consuela. I didn't know she'd left."

"You might check your den. Maybe she left a note for you there. Mine was in my room."

Drew was through the kitchen door before the housekeeper had finished talking. He picked up the blue envelope he found under the door and ripped it open. *Dear Drew, Thanks for your gracious hospitality. Sincerely, Sunny.* He crumpled it in his hand and threw it at the wastebasket. He crossed the den quickly and went into Sunny's room.

The room was empty, sterile. He opened the drawers, the closet. She was gone. Even the wheelchair was gone. She'd done a thorough job. He went into the bathroom. He could smell the scent of her in here. Her body . . . her shampoo . . . He swung the door shut and slammed his fist against it.

The hit was muffled by fabric. He looked up. On the hook hung her white cotton gown. The white gown she'd worn in the hospital. The gown he'd slowly unbuttoned and slid from her quivering body.

He clutched the gown in his hands. A deep, guttural sound ripped from the depths of his soul. He buried his face in the fabric, inhaling the essence of her scent. Memories flashed across his mind. His heart grieved and his body hardened. Drew leaned back against the bathroom counter, his face buried in Sunny's gown, choking back sobs—sobs he reined in with the sheer force of his will. His chest ached with the effort. He buried the sobs and the pain in the deep, empty well he called his life. He buried them under the ripping pain and under the haunting memories.

Sunny awakened slowly. Her eyes burned. She looked around, recognizing her own room. Memories pounded through her skull. She rolled onto her side, pulling herself into a tight fetal position. She groaned, attempting to ease her pain with a slight rocking motion.

Sunny heard the phone ring. Once. Twice. Three times. It stopped. She turned her electric blanket up. She was cold, so very cold. She knew it would take a lot more than an electric blanket to warm her. She glanced at the clock. It was still early. Her mouth tasted like something unmentionable. Probably the brandy she'd had in the middle of the night. It had been worth the slow trip downstairs and then back upstairs to get the desired effect. She'd been able to relax a little and drift off for a couple of hours of oblivion.

Sunny opened her eyes again and looked around her room. With a flick of the bedspread, she'd thrown everything off her bed last night, and now she looked at the boxes. The delicate fabrics spilled from them, taunting her with her failure to win the man with whom she wanted to spend the rest of her life.

She felt angry and scared and hopelessly in love. She had empty arms and a heart too full. Rolling onto her back, she let the pain coil through her, almost needing it. Maybe it would be a catharsis; maybe the pain would bring her back to her senses.

Sunny had been certain that if she persisted, Drew would come to love her, and he had, but he wouldn't allow it to make a difference. For the first time, the goal she'd set for herself was unattainable. It was not within her power to achieve it. Sadly, she understood she couldn't always reach out and take what she wanted.

Defeat was bitter. Bitter beyond belief. Drew had thrown up the one defensive wall she had no way of scaling—his perception of himself. Only he could change that.

Drew put the phone down. He didn't know what he'd have said if she'd answered. But he had to know that she was all right.

He dialed Mike's number. "Mike, this is Drew."

"What time is it?" Mike asked as he stretched to reach his alarm clock.

"Morning."

"Couldn't tell it by me."

"Just wake up, will you? I need a favor."

His brother's tone reached through Mike's sleep-dulled brain. Wide-awake, Mike sat up in bed. "What's wrong?"

Drew cleared his throat twice, fighting to get the words beyond his pride. "I need you to go over and check on her. She went home last night." The line was silent.

"We're talking about Sunny, I assume?"

"Yes."

"What the hell is going on, Drew? What did you do?"

"Never mind that. Would you please just go over and check on her? See if she needs groceries or anything."

"I thought you two were getting along great. I even thought there was something between you. You're perfect for each other."

"Please, Mike, I don't want to talk about it."

Drew sounded rather desperate, an emotion Mike had rarely, if ever, heard from his older sibling. "I've got time before my shift. I'll go."

"Call me. Call me as soon as you leave her."

When the doorbell rang, Sunny groaned and pulled herself into a tighter ball. It was barely dawn, and she didn't want to see anyone—no one, not even Drew. But after another moment of noise, she knew she had no choice but to get up.

Gathering her crutches under her arms, she walked to the window that overlooked the front of the house and immediately recognized Mike's Mustang. She groaned aloud. Unlocking the window, Sunny pushed it open.

"Go away, Mike."

"So you are alive, although you hardly look it."

"I don't want company."

"I'm not company. I'm your friend. Come on down, Sunny, and unlock the door. I'm not leaving until I've talked to you."

She knew it was useless to argue. With a sigh of exasperation, Sunny slammed the window shut and made her way downstairs.

Mike closed the door behind him and leaned against it. He caught a glimpse of her swollen and pale face before she ducked her head. She'd evidently slept in her clothes. He saw her shiver. The place felt as cold as the North Pole.

He reached for her, and Sunny let her crutches clatter to the floor, throwing herself into Mike's arms. The tears she'd thought long gone came anew.

When the sobs eased, Mike picked her up and carried her to the sofa. Propping her in the corner since she didn't look as if she had the strength or the will to sit up on her own, he went to the thermostat and turned it up. Glancing at Sunny, her head in her arms on the arm of the sofa, he walked to the kitchen to start coffee. Mike came back into the hall to look at her a couple of times while the coffee brewed, but she hadn't moved. He didn't think she was asleep. Pouring two large mugs of coffee, he sat down beside her.

The house had begun to warm a bit, and Sunny stopped shivering, but she avoided Mike's look as she took the coffee. "What's going on, Sunny? You shouldn't be here by yourself."

She shrugged her shoulders and took a sip of coffee.

"Drew called me before dawn and asked me to come over and check on you." He had her attention now. She looked at him, then glanced away. The pain in her eyes was obvious, and hard for him to deal with. Damn Drew! Her hands trembled on the mug, but Mike knew it wasn't from the cold. He reached over and steadied it for her.

"You and Drew seem so right for each other. I really thought the two of you would click."

Sunny blinked and swallowed as tears formed and slid down her cheeks. "We did. We really did."

"Tell me what happened, Sun." Mike watched her shake her head slowly as another tear rolled down her cheek and dripped off her chin. She seemed unaware of the tears as she stared into her almost empty coffee cup.

"I've never felt so helpless."

"What do you mean?"

"Get my crutches for me, Mike. I need to go to the bathroom. I'm going to be sick."

Mike dialed the ranch. His brother answered before the end of the first ring. "Damn you, Drew! What have you done to her? I should never have let you get within a million miles of her."

"I told you I didn't want her here. Is she all right?"

"Hell, no. I think you better level with me about what's going on, and her name's Sunny. Can't you say it?"

Drew ignored Mike. "What did she tell you?"

"Nothing really. She just cries. She looks awful, and

I can hear her in the bathroom throwing up. Does that make you feel better, big bro? Why don't you get your butt down here and take care of her?''

"Does she need a doctor?"

Hearing Sunny open the bathroom door, Mike said, "I'll talk to you later." He hung up the phone as Sunny came into the room.

"I've got to be at the station in twenty minutes. After my shift, I'll stop and pick up some groceries for you. Anything in particular you want?"

Sunny shook her head. "Who were you talking to?"

After a moment, Mike answered, "Drew." Mike watched pain flash across her face again. "If it would help, I'd beat him up for you." Mike watched a ghost of a smile tug at her lips.

"You're sweet. Why couldn't Drew have been more like you?"

Mike's comeback was quick and honest. "Because then you wouldn't have fallen in love with him. Right?"

Sunny glanced away from Mike's questioning look and nodded.

After a moment of poignant silence, Mike asked, "Can I get you anything or help you get upstairs?"

"I'll be okay. I can get up and down the stairs without too much trouble. I did it a couple of times at . . . at the ranch."

"What were you doing upstairs?" When he saw her pale further, Mike said, "Never mind, I don't think I want to know."

Mike longed to give Sunny a bit of hope, but knowing his brother, he figured sympathy was what she would be needing.

THIRTEEN

For once, Gus didn't glance at the guard, nor did he check the clock on the dingy gray wall. Relaxed, he tipped back on his chair, looking first at Mason and then at Rob. "This will be our last time here to finalize plans. What's been happening where you are, Rob?"

"Nothing really. There's a police dog on the ranch now. He's evidently been trained. The dog hates me. He belongs to the woman who's staying there. I pulled that information out of the lieutenant's kid."

"Okay. Be certain you don't leave any kind of evidence behind. Clear out anything personal, but leave your ranch clothes—whatever you purchased for the job, anything anyone has seen you use. But don't leave anything which can be traced to you—or me. On your next day off, sell the truck to a used-car dealer or, if you can, privately. Tell anyone at the ranch that you had to leave it in the shop."

"Mason, make certain you time the phone call right. We don't want to lure him up there too early. I don't want any evidence left on the land—only the crop. Double-check. Clear out in two days."

"There's not a flaw in the plan," Mason stated.

"Remember, I don't want either of you anywhere near that crop. Just make the phone calls and get the hell out of the area. The sheriff will take it from there." Gus hugged his brothers before the armed guard led him away.

For days sleep had eluded Sunny, and when she did nap from exhaustion, she was awakened with erotic dreams that left her in such a state of need, she couldn't drift off again. She tried to eat, yet very little food would move past the lump in her throat.

How could she have been so naive as to think Drew would simply fall in love with her, and they would live happily ever after? She couldn't believe how arrogant she'd been in proposing and expecting him to answer yes. She now realized she'd disregarded the signals he'd given—his aloofness and his unapproachability. She'd barged ahead, striving to be successful one more time, as if he were one of her tangible goals. But this time the goal had been beyond her grasp.

She'd wanted to share the good and bad with Drew for a lifetime—she'd wanted the give and take—a word of praise, a squeeze of the hand on a black day.

Now she felt as though there were nothing left of her, no heart, no gut, nothing—no cohesive substance to hold her life together. She'd gone past the embarrassment, beyond the humiliation, past the anger and the despair. There was only a hollow ache where the happiness and pleasure had been such a short time ago. The love that had blossomed was still there; it would always be a part of who she was. The only tears left were the ones in her heart—the ones no one could see.

Sunny knew life had to go on, but her zest for life had diminished. She and Mike were going out to dinner tomorrow with friends to celebrate her recovery. She'd do her best to act her usual cheerful self. Yet she knew, given the choice, she'd take the pain of a broken ankle any day over the agony of a freshly broken heart.

She had stripped herself bare before Drew. Holding nothing back, she had offered everything to him—her love, her virginity, the very essence of who she was. She'd offered to share it with him for a lifetime of love. She loved him totally and without restraint, yet he hadn't taken a heartbeat to consider what she was offering, what she was asking. He'd simply refused with about as much emotion as one would show when refusing dessert. Her husband hunt had been short-lived. She'd found him. She'd lost him. She'd never look again.

Drew paced. Exhausted. He hadn't gotten a decent night's sleep in a week. Thoughts of Sunny robbed him of the peace he'd thought he had achieved. He rubbed the back of his neck and then raked his fingers through his hair, which badly needed a cut. But he didn't seem to care about much of anything right now.

The house was so quiet. It felt cold like a tomb, his personal tomb, without her warmth. Rico whined because she wasn't around to play games with him. Consuela treated him as if he'd committed first-degree murder, and Mike was angry. His brother was acting as if he owned her, and Drew resented that greatly. For the first time in years, they'd thrown angry words at each other.

Mike had not minced any words this morning, either. He'd been very direct and told Drew if he wanted to know anything about her, he was going to either have to call her or drive to Albuquerque to see her. The thing was, he didn't want to talk to her or see her; he simply needed to know she was all right, but his brother wouldn't even give him that much information.

She had infuriated him. She had aroused him. She'd made him laugh. She'd done so much more than satisfy his physical craving. Sunny had reached in and touched him emotionally, filling a deep loneliness no one else had ever touched.

He picked up the phone and started punching in her number. There was a void in his life now. But wait, wasn't that what he'd been waiting for? For her to leave his home? For her to get the hell out of his life? Well, she was gone. He slammed down the phone, hating himself. He couldn't say her name. How could he? The sunshine that had briefly illuminated his existence had disappeared from his life.

He didn't know how long he sat there staring at tomorrow's date on the calendar. The day she was to have her cast cut off. The appointment would involve minor surgery to remove one of the screws that had held her ankle in place for healing. Then she would be able to put weight on her foot and begin to walk again.

He did know he couldn't let her face it alone. He lifted the phone from its cradle and slowly pushed each digit of her number. The melodious tone of her voice washed over him. "Drew here." He didn't pause. He didn't want her to have the opportunity to hang up on him. "I'll be there tomorrow in plenty of time to take you to your appointment." Before she could respond, he broke the connection.

The next morning Drew rang the bell and glanced at his watch. He'd tried to time this so he wouldn't be too early—early enough for a lengthy conversation—or too late—late enough that she would worry.

Hearing the click of the dead bolt, he watched the door open. Through the screen door he could see she'd lost weight. The sparkle in her eyes had faded.

"Come in for a minute. I thought maybe you'd bring Prince down with you."

"I would have, but I didn't have Dramamine for

him, so I was afraid to chance it.'' He followed her inside and closed the door, leaning against it.

"I need to get my jacket.'' When Sunny returned, she had her jacket on and keys in her hand. "Thanks for coming to take me. I'd planned to call a cab.''

Drew nodded. "I wanted to do this for you, to make it easier. But please don't misunderstand. . . . This doesn't change anything. Nothing's changed since we last spoke.''

Sunny studied his face, then nodded. It was obvious to her he'd gone to battle with himself, and his demeanor stated they'd both lost. "I realize that.''

Still on crutches, Sunny accompanied Dr. Johnson out to the room where Drew waited. She watched him stand as she came toward him.

"Lieutenant. You're looking good.''

"Doctor.'' He nodded in recognition, but his eyes were only for Sunny. He glanced down at her leg. "How does it feel?''

"Good, thank you. And very light.''

Dr. Johnson glanced between the two and said, "Give it time to heal, Sunny. Don't push it, and come back to see me before you decide to try jogging again.''

Sunny was quiet as Drew walked beside her to his car and got in. He reached for his sunglasses and put them on. He turned sideways in the seat. "Why don't we stop and have lunch before I drive you home?''

Sunny glanced across the car at him. The same car that weeks ago had taken her to Santa Fe had brought her full circle. So much had happened, yet so little had actually changed in her life. His eyes were once again hidden behind the reflective lenses. She sadly wondered if Drew would always hide from the world. She recognized it was no longer her concern. "Thanks for the thought, but I'd rather just go home.''

Drew studied her. This was a different person than

he'd ever seen. This Sunny was remote and taciturn. This Sunny had lost her zest for living. As he fired the powerful engine of the car and drove toward her home, Drew acknowledged to himself that he had no one to blame but himself for the changes.

After unlocking the front door, she turned toward him, wishing she could see beyond the reflective lenses and into his soul. She couldn't. "Thanks for the ride. Please give Consuela my regards and tell Rico I'll be up in a few days to get Prince." Sunny stepped over the threshold and shut the door.

Drew stood unmoving, staring at the closed door before he turned and walked to his car.

Sunny didn't glance back at the closed door and the man who stood on the other side. She understood the finality of refusing his invitation.

She walked straight to the kitchen. She had a new goal—to walk without crutches. She leaned the crutches in the corner and, holding on to the counter, tried to put weight on her left foot. Her ankle rebelled with pain and stiffness, but she persisted, forcing it into motion, desperately trying not to give in to the limp.

According to the doctor, only time would give the final prognosis. Now all she had to do was walk. And walk she would. Back and forth, the length of the kitchen. Back and forth, hobbling in a halting, jerking gait. She could begin to work her ankle, begin to walk again, begin to jog again . . . and jog she would. If only she could jog at least five miles right now, she could replace the terrible emptiness she felt with exhaustion, and then perhaps she could get a full night of sleep.

Sunny planned to be walking within days. She made the decision she wouldn't go and get Prince until she could walk without the crutches. Her father would be home within a few days. She'd be back to work in another week. Life would go on.

FOURTEEN

Sunny brushed the short crop of her hair. She liked the new style—it suited her. The cut gave her a chic, free-spirited look. Free. She sobered for a moment and closed her eyes against the sudden flash of pain—free for a lifetime. She opened her eyes and smiled at her reflection in the vanity mirror. "You're one tough lady, a survivor, and don't ever forget it."

Sunny glanced one last time at herself. She snorted at the irony. Her transformation was complete. Finally. But now it was for herself. She didn't want to remember—not that she wouldn't look back and reminisce, especially about the good times she'd shared with Drew—but not now, not until her pain had eased.

She felt good about herself. Oh, yes, an intrinsic part of her was missing. Somehow she recognized that the love she felt for Drew was a once-in-a-lifetime love. But she'd arrived at a significant conclusion—she could live without him. Drew was not essential to her existence. She was complete within herself.

She pulled the suede blazer on over the tailored slacks and blouse. Tugging on the leather boots, she winced. Her ankle was quite swollen, but most of the pain had vanished and only the stiffness remained. She wouldn't be able to spend hours walking yet or even jog a half mile, but she was walking without a limp. It would be good to have Prince back. She'd begin by walking him, and they'd work up to a jog together.

She'd talked to Rico last night and thanked him for taking care of the dog. Anxious to get Prince, she glanced at her watch. She needed to get on the road, because her father was coming home late this afternoon, and she wanted to be at the airport in plenty of time. They would have the weekend together before she started work on Monday.

"Is this Lieutenant Drew Williams?"

Drew frowned, then answered. "Speaking."

"The sheriff is on his way to your ranch. Your operation has been discovered. The one up on the northern border of your property. Close to the county road—about a mile west. Congratulations, Lieutenant! You've been framed."

The phone disconnected. Dial tone. Drew took the receiver from his ear and looked at it. His mind rushed to recall the voice. He didn't recognize it, but he concluded he might have if it hadn't been disguised. He sat at his desk, his body coiled tight, filtering the information from the call for clues. Evidently feeling his tension, Prince whined. Drew scratched him behind the ears.

Framed! Who could be behind this, or was it a means to lure him there? He stood. "Come on, Prince. We're going for a ride. Hope you know your manners around a horse."

Drew walked to the kitchen, Prince trailing at his heels. "Consuela, did you recognize the voice of that caller?"

"His voice? Didn't you find out who it was? Didn't you talk to him?"

"Yeah, I talked to him. I'm going to ride up toward the county road and check things out. I'm taking Prince with me."

"But Sunny's coming to get him."

"Then she'll have to wait a few minutes. If I'm not back by one, get ahold of Charlie and tell him to come up there."

"Is something wrong?"

"I really don't know. That was one weird phone call. Something about the sheriff had been called and would be going up there. The caller gave me specific directions. Said I'd been framed."

"Framed? Where should I tell Charlie to go? Better put it on paper. You know how I am about directions."

Drew took a pencil and paper from the drawer and sketched a quick map.

"Do you want the dog's leash?"

"No, I'm riding the stallion. It will be just as quick. I'd like to approach the area without being seen or heard and find out if anything's going on before I show myself."

"Don't you think you should call the sheriff?"

"According to the mystery man, he's already been called. Tell Sunny to wait. I shouldn't be too long."

An hour later, Sunny pulled to a stop on the gravel drive and took a deep breath. Drew's Bronco was parked beside the house. She shrugged her shoulders. She studied the home in front of her dispassionately, refusing to recall the day she'd arrived here with Drew weeks ago. If she could refuse his invitation to lunch and close the door in his face, then she could deal with him today, and once again walk away and be all the stronger for it.

It was cold, but the sun shone brilliantly. She glanced at her watch. She had plenty of time to give Prince his medication, drink a cup of coffee with Consuela, and get back to Albuquerque to pick up her father. Sunny frowned as she rang the bell again. The door was unlocked.

"Sunny? I'm in the kitchen on the phone." Consuela covered the phone and spoke as she entered the room, "You look super. You're walking! I'm trying to reach Charlie. They've evidently got problems with a mare in foal, but Drew wanted him to come up to the northern border of the property if he wasn't back by now. Charlie says he can't go for at least another hour."

"Where's Prince?"

"Drew went on horseback and took the dog with him."

"What's going on? Didn't he know I was coming today?"

"I don't really know what's happening. He had a phone call, and Drew said something was wrong and that if he didn't show up by one at the latest, I'd better send Charlie."

Sunny glanced at her watch. She couldn't wait too long since she didn't want to miss her father's plane. If Drew didn't come back shortly, she'd go find them. "I wonder why he took Prince when he knew I was coming to get him."

Drew shook his head, remembering the last time he'd ridden Black Devil. Had he come this far on the horse that day? He wasn't certain. He did remember the emotional turmoil that had surfaced within him then. Quickly covering the miles on the stallion, he was flooded with memories—memories of them together in his bed, in her bed. Memories of her smile, of her scent. Sunny—the last time he'd seen her, she'd said no and closed the door in his face. The thought of seeing her soon tightened his gut.

Drew, the stallion, and Prince topped the last ridge half an hour later. Taking the field glasses from the saddlebag, he surveyed the area. He was still about half a mile from the designated location, but he didn't see the sheriff's car or any other. A car would have stuck out like a sore thumb in the rolling red hills and the contrasting greens of the piñons and junipers. He frowned and looked around. Prince lifted his nose and sniffed the air.

He was following an elusive trail. Drew reviewed the phone call again. His mind told him he wasn't crazy for coming. His instincts told him something was going down, and he preferred to observe from a distance and not become an uninformed participant. He glanced at his watch. He'd been here for more than an hour.

Drew moved along the ridge another quarter mile, staying close to the low-growing trees, in the shadows. He again commanded the dog to stay as he closed his eyes to rest them from the brilliant sunlight. When he opened them, he thought he saw movement out of the corner of his eye. Taking the binoculars, he scanned the terrain. Nothing. He slowly searched the area again. He stopped. He sat astride the stallion, absolutely still, watching. He caught a movement in the trees, close to the road. Someone was there.

Now that they'd meandered down through the trees and were within a quarter mile of the area, Prince was becoming agitated.

Drew pulled the glasses away from his eyes and listened. He could hear the sound of a vehicle in the distance. Well concealed in the shadows, he waited to see who would arrive.

His vantage point wasn't as good as earlier when he'd been up on the ridge, but he focused the glasses a bit. The color was wrong for this time of year . . . too green. Some type of crop had been planted in the area. Drew squinted. If his guess was right, it was marijuana—not well developed, but marijuana. Damn! Probably over half an acre, growing on his property.

Under ideal conditions, the street value of such a crop would be significant. Obviously a frame. Without taking his gaze from the area in front of him, he reached down and reassured himself the rifle was in the scabbard.

The sound of the vehicle grew louder, and a moment later, nothing—silence. It wasn't Charlie. He would have driven his four-wheel drive right into the area where Drew had drawn the map. Probably the sheriff.

Sunny stopped her car. The road was too rough to go on. She glanced at the map Consuela had given her. Stepping from the car, she glanced around and slowly walked up the rutted road. Maybe Drew and Prince had already headed back. She'd walk up the road a short distance and see if she saw them.

Drew straightened in the saddle and squinted into the binoculars. The glint of red-gold hair . . . Sunny! What the hell was she doing up here? Couldn't she ever do as he asked? He lifted the binoculars and watched her walk up the road, disappearing around a bend. Walking slowly but on her own. His shoulders sagged in relief. Damn, she'd cropped her hair off short. At the sight of her, fragments of memories and scents and feelings raced through him with the speed of a windblown brush fire.

The memories stopped as abruptly as they'd begun as he again caught movement in his peripheral vision. Nudging the horse into a walk, Drew raised the binoculars. Movement—this time he could see someone hurrying from tree to tree, moving in Sunny's direction.

Prince picked up her scent and began a low-pitched whine. Drew silenced the dog with a hand signal and a quiet command to keep him from rushing forward. Drew sat like a statue in the saddle, refusing to move a muscle. His thoughts raced, listing options, tossing them aside like so much confetti in the wind. He didn't want to give away his position, yet he wanted to rush forward. He took a deep breath.

He swung the lenses up to his eyes again and felt for the rifle with his other hand. Moving down the incline as silently and quickly as possible, he kept the binoculars to his eyes. He debated with himself even as he continued down the rocky slope—move in quickly, or hang back to see what developed? He wasn't going to know exactly where Sunny was or what kind of trouble she was in until he rode into the middle of it.

He wanted to move into the open and try to pick up the sight of her again. He wanted to race down the hill and force the situation. He wanted to protect her at all costs. He loved her. He urged the horse forward. If a sheriff was supposed to be here, why wasn't he? His instinct told him whoever was in the area spelled trouble. The person didn't want to be seen and had done a good job evading his watch. His gut told him to rush, his logic said to keep his presence unknown until he knew what was happening. But with Sunny in the area, his options had narrowed.

A high-pitched whistle rent the air. Drew's stomach rolled as he heard the whistle of a mistress calling her dog. Prince offered a sharp bark of response and launched down the side of the mountain, darting between the trees, leaving dust in his trail.

Drew realized his error. He should have moved in sooner to see who was in the area. He was at a distinct disadvantage. Sunny, *his* Sunny, was in danger.

A haunting scream brought his rushing thoughts to a fast conclusion. The decision had been made, yet still he had no choice but to move with caution. If anything, he had to move with more caution now—Sunny's life could depend on it. He tightened his hand on the reins, and the horse stopped.

When the silence continued, he pulled the binoculars

to his eyes. He could see the edge of the crop. Definitely marijuana. Damn. Someone was attempting to frame him, and now Sunny had stumbled into the trap.

The horse tossed his head at the sound of a shout and Prince's bark. His own gut twisted as he silently stopped at the edge of the small clearing. Rob Farley. Drew let the binoculars fall onto his chest and reached for the rifle. There was no way to circle around and come in on Farley's back side.

With gut-wrenching clarity, Drew realized he'd made a massive error when he'd shoved Sunny away, when he'd refused her proposal and crushed the offer of her love into the ground. He wanted to love her for a lifetime.

Farley. Damn! Why hadn't he followed his instincts about the man and fired him weeks ago? The man held Sunny in front of him, twisting and turning in different directions as Prince was ready to launch himself at Farley the first opportunity he had. But Farley kept the dog at bay with Sunny's body held tight against his own.

Drew rode straight into the clearing, drawing Farley's attention away from the dog for a moment. Drew kept his eyes on Farley, never daring to glance directly at Sunny, yet aware of how her hands clawed at the grip he had on her neck. Drew had no choice but to keep his cool. Farley had Sunny, and consequently the upper hand. With one good jerk he could break her neck. Drew only hoped Sunny didn't realize it.

Fear for Sunny tore through him. Drew wanted to tear Farley limb from limb. He only had a rifle, which he knew he'd never use with Sunny in the man's grip. This man, whom he'd always disliked, now held Sunny like a boa constrictor about to squeeze its prey to death.

Drew realized if he made one minute error in judgment, either in what he said or how he commanded Prince, Sunny's life would be in grave danger. He recognized her very life depended on him and him alone. If he could distract Farley's attention and Sunny could get away, Prince could more than handle the man.

Drew stopped a few feet in back of Prince and lowered the rifle.

"Ha. If it isn't the hotshot lieutenant come calling." The man spoke in a breathy voice. He was winded from avoiding Prince. "See what a tasty morsel I found for myself. Did she come to rescue you? Toss that rifle to the ground, then get off that horse, slowly. No sudden movements."

While Farley talked, Drew sorted alternatives in his mind, not finding an acceptable solution. Knowing he had no choice at this point but to follow Farley's directives, Drew tossed the rifle behind him. His mind fought to disregard the woman Farley held. If she was to survive unharmed, he had room for only two focal points in his mind—Prince and Farley.

Drew eased out of the saddle, not trusting his knee to support him—but knowing he had no choice. He walked slowly toward the dog and stood a few feet from Farley and Sunny.

"Nice crop you've got here, Farley. You grow this stuff in the Dakotas, too? Little undernourished, wouldn't you say? I don't really think it's going to reach maturation—it's getting a bit too cold. What are you going to do for money then?"

Farley laughed. "Oh well, your loss. The point wasn't to harvest the crop—just show the sheriff what you're up to. He should be here any time. Glad you could make it on time."

"And when the sheriff does show, Farley, how are you going to explain why you're holding the former chief of police's daughter hostage?"

"She's insurance to keep that flea-bitten monster off me."

"Are you such a weakling you're going to hide behind a woman's skirts? This nice shepherd . . . what could he do to you?''

"Nice my foot. Whenever he comes within a mile of me, he's ready to take a bite. Never known a mutt who wouldn't eat meat.''

"How'd you get here, Farley?'' Drew looked around for the truck that had been at the ranch. "Who's responsible for this? Certainly not a weakling like you.'' Drew watched Farley tense. Drew knew he was playing with fire, but words were all he had to test what Farley would and could do. He was the only one who could pull this guy's death grip from around Sunny's neck. He couldn't charge the guy, and he couldn't command Prince to either. Somehow he knew this would depend on the ability of his mind, not his body. Somehow he knew it would be enough. He just prayed he would play Farley right and not push him to harm her further.

"Someone bigger than you is behind this. Someone with a lot more guts than you, a lot smarter than you. I would even bet you're not supposed to be here. You've really blown it, haven't you? A frame would only work in your absence. Are you going to take the rap for this crop?'' He saw Farley's grip tighten on Sunny, and a funny little noise emitted from her throat. Drew's heart wrenched, but he ignored the sound and pushed his advantage. "Did you plant it? When? On the weekends? Some big daddy paying you a few measly bucks to try to frame me?

"You're not too smart if you think anybody's going to believe this. I know every lawman in the area. Maybe if you hadn't come with the deal. Maybe if you weren't standing here with a hostage.''

He let his glance slide away from Farley to check Prince. The dog's teeth were bared, and the low growl never stopped. Drew listened. "Popular place. Maybe that's your boss looking for you, Robbie.''

"Shut up or I'll kill her. And don't call me that.''

"Well, well." Drew glanced over and saw the sheriff's car. "It's the sheriff who's come calling for your hide, Robbie. Aren't you the one who called him? How convenient for you to show up for your own arrest. You are truly stupid, Robbie."

Drew could see he had him rattled. He could practically smell the man's fear. Seeing the fright in the man's eyes, Drew raised his hand, attracting Prince's attention.

The sound of car doors distracted Farley, and he loosened his grip on Sunny. The man glanced over to see the sheriff step out of his car. It was all the distraction Drew needed.

Even as he moved toward her, he shouted, "Move, Sunny, get the hell out of the way."

Suddenly free, Sunny closed her eyes and gasped for air.

Farley ran for the stallion, managing to get one foot in the stirrup as Prince latched on to his leg. Black Devil shied and reared, lunging forward. Drew rushed toward Sunny and yanked her out of the way of the horse's hooves. Drew's gaze touched her briefly before he pulled her into his arms.

Drew watched as Farley, his foot caught in the stirrup, was dragged.

Sunny stood, clinging to Drew, dragging shuddering breaths of air into her starving lungs.

Bracing himself to hold her up, Drew held Sunny away from him and studied her. "Are you hurt?"

Sunny shook her head even as she touched her throat. Drew reached up and caressed her neck with his fingers.

They were both distracted by the sheriff. "Drew, how do you want to deal with this horse? He doesn't want me approaching him."

With one last glance, Drew released Sunny and went to quiet the horse, which pawed the ground in an agitated state. Sunny stood right behind him as Drew released the unconscious man's twisted foot from the stirrup.

Sunny knelt over the inert form and felt for a pulse. Prince whined at her shoulder. "Good boy, Prince," she crooned.

"Drew. What's this all about? Had the strangest call a while ago. Told the boys I'd check it out myself."

"I don't know who the hell he is, but he's been working on my ranch under the name of Rob Farley." Drew swung his arm in the direction of the crop of marijuana. "Admitted this was planted to frame me. I never found out who he's working for. Charlie, my foreman, hired him a while back. His references checked out, but something obviously got past us."

"Check for an ID and I'll call for assistance."

FIFTEEN

Sunny felt Drew's scrutiny occasionally, but after help arrived, the authorities demanded his total attention. She watched as Farley was loaded into the helicopter to be airlifted to the hospital in Albuquerque. The horse had dragged him quite a way. He had sustained a head injury and was unconscious. Her guess was that he'd come out of it in a few hours. Turning, she felt Prince nudge her side. She realized Drew was immersed in details with the sheriff, trying to determine Farley's actual identity and who had instigated the frame.

Brushing the dirt off her clothing, she gave Prince a pat on the head and, not bothering to talk to anyone, walked toward her car. Her ankle hurt like the devil from all the walking, and it had been twisted several times while Farley had held her. She tamped down the remnant of fear as she touched her neck. Reaching her car, Sunny started the motor. Not noticing Prince's whine as he licked at her tears, Sunny drove toward Albuquerque. Her father's plane had landed hours ago, and she knew he would be worried about her.

She drove, trying to erase from her mind all the

trauma she'd faced—erase the image of the man she loved. She had her dog. Wasn't that what she'd come for?

Sunny blinked at the tears as a car beside her honked. She couldn't remember leaving the ranch, turning onto the southbound freeway, or wandering into the other lane. Pulling back into her own lane, she realized she was at the northern edge of the city.

Arriving home a few minutes later, she drove into the garage, thankful for the door opener. She closed it behind her and slumped on the steering wheel, wishing for the oblivion of sleep, wanting to escape thought and memories.

"Sunny, is that you?" her father asked.

She opened the car door and shakily stood, holding on to the doorframe. "Welcome home, Dad. Sorry I didn't make it to the airport." She offered him a watery smile. "I've missed you." She put her arms around him, swallowing her tears.

Loosening her hug, he looked at her. "My God, where have you been? I've been worried about you. I've got some news for you, but let's get you into the house." Joe turned on the overhead light in the garage. "Were you in an accident?"

"I'm okay, really. I want to take a bath and lie down for a while. It's been a long day."

Joe frowned at his daughter but put his arm around her waist. Upon closer inspection, he lifted her in his arms and carried her through the house and up the stairs, setting her carefully on the bed. He knelt in front of her and pulled off her boots. He held the one foot in his hand. "Your ankle's terribly swollen." He glanced up at her. "What happened to your neck?"

She focused on her father's worried face. "I'm all right. Everything turned out fine. I'll be downstairs in a while and tell you about it."

"You've lost weight. A slight breeze could topple you over."

"I'll be okay, really. I can't tell you how glad I am to have you home." Sunny stood and made her way to the bathroom, closing the door with finality.

Joe left the room when he heard the sound of water running in the tub. He frowned. Sunny had changed in a fundamental way since he'd left for Australia.

Joe glanced at the clock again. She'd been asleep for more than an hour. He listened to another news brief concerning Drew. Someone had tried to frame him, but the details were still sketchy. He would tell Sunny when she awakened. Thank God this hadn't happened while she'd been staying there.

When the doorbell rang, Joe jumped up from his recliner, where he'd been awaiting the evening news.

"Drew. Good to see you after all this time. Thanks for taking Sunny in while I was away." Joe reached out to pump his hand. "You really are okay. I've been watching the news. What happened? Who was the woman this man held hostage? Anyone you know?"

Drew looked at him and frowned. Joe didn't know. "Where's Sunny? I need to see her."

"She's asleep. Sit down and let's look at the news." They glanced at the television.

"We now have an update on an earlier story. Ms. Sunny Steele was held hostage on Lieutenant Drew Williams' ranch. . . ."

Joe turned and glared at Drew as the reporter droned on about the event. "Is that where she was? She came home looking dead on her feet. What happened? Has she been checked by a doctor? She wouldn't talk to me. She insisted on taking a bath, and when I went up to check on her, she was asleep."

"Easy, Joe. Sunny's okay. Right now I need to see her, to talk to her."

When Joe hesitated, Drew said, "Joe, trust me on this one. I'm not going to hurt her. I love your daughter."

Joe frowned and studied the man in front of him. Drew had been one of his best lieutenants. A man he'd trust with his life. But Sunny had lost weight. The sparkle had disappeared from her eyes. Besides the hostage situation she'd been party to, as her father, he instinctively knew there was something else wrong. The two men faced off as if ready to duel, staring at each other, each taking the other's measure. Joe finally acquiesced with a nod. "I'll take your word on that."

"Thanks, Joe. You won't regret it." He shook Joe's hand. Drew took the stairs one at a time, slowly, his knee protesting with the jar of each step. His heart thundered in his chest. He wanted her so much. He'd been afraid when she'd disappeared after Farley had been loaded into the helicopter. He'd walked down the rutted road, ignoring the reporters who had dogged his footsteps.

He opened her bedroom door and closed it behind him. The room was dark except for the light from the bathroom. She breathed deeply. Exhaustion and shock had taken their toll. Her skin was pale. Under her eyes, the shadows were dark against her translucent skin.

He was glad now he'd forced himself to shower and change before racing down here. He watched her sleep as he had so many nights when she'd first arrived at his home.

Sadness squeezed his heart as he remembered how he'd hurt her with his words and how he'd refused her proposal. She'd offered the kind of love most men would die for, and he'd refused it so casually, as if the opportunity for a love like that were given to him any time he wanted it.

Walking to the side of the bed, Drew reached down, his fingers touching the softness of her hair. He loved the color; he didn't know what to think about the new style. He wanted to cherish this moment, but he also wanted to awaken her.

Drew saw things he'd not had time to notice earlier. She'd lost even more weight. Her face had a gaunt look, and the circles under her eyes spoke of little sleep. He tugged on the blanket and covered her bare shoulder.

He wanted to strip and crawl in bed beside her, hold her body against his own, and let her sleep until she was totally rested; then . . . they'd go on to other things . . . talking . . . loving. . . . But he didn't move toward the bed. Instead, he lifted an antique chair that couldn't have been made for comfort, and placed it near the bed. Lowering himself onto the chair, he propped his feet on the edge of the bed and waited.

The aftereffects of the adrenaline still flowed through his body. He was wound tight, yet he sat motionless, his gaze fixed on Sunny. He ignored the peal of the doorbell time and again, and he finally unplugged the extension of the phone on the desk across the room so it wouldn't disturb her.

He knew Joe was adept at handling the reporters, who wanted a story—always after a story. Didn't they understand there were more important things than a story? There were hurts to mend, lives to plan. But Sunny slept, unaware of the man who could not take his eyes from her.

He'd realized so much this afternoon when he'd recognized how close he'd come to losing her. Since Sunny's proposal, he'd learned a tremendous amount about himself. Her words had never been far from his mind. She'd forced him to take a new look at himself. She'd said what no one else had the nerve to tell him. She'd seen through his rationalizations, and because she loved him, she'd had the courage to tell him and then to walk away. His handicap *was* in his mind. His view of himself had ruptured their relationship. He only hoped it wasn't too late to ask her forgiveness.

And this afternoon, when he'd seen her at Farley's mercy, his life had been put in perspective. His disability was a small factor. He could handle that. There would always be things he wouldn't be able to do, things he would want to do, like backpacking with Rico. But that wasn't what had kept him from loving Sunny, from responding to her love.

It had been his own bitter pride. He'd swallowed his pride this afternoon like bitter, green bile and rid himself of the emotional baggage he'd carried for far too long. He'd gone from the fear of any kind of emotional entanglement to wanting a lifetime of commitment with her. Someday he would try to explain everything to her, but for now he just wanted the chance to ask her forgiveness and ask for the privilege of sharing his life with her.

When Sunny stirred, a soft moan escaped her parted lips. She'd never felt so tired. She fought against wakening, wanting, for a reason she was unable to discern at the moment, the oblivion of sleep. She frowned as memories inundated her consciousness.

She groaned again and pushed at her hair. She heard the creak of the old chair that sat across the room, but it sounded much closer, and she opened her eyes a bit. The bright afternoon sun had disappeared, and the room was almost dark. Someone had pulled the drapes. She must have slept for several hours. She sat up, and the comforter drifted down, baring her breasts.

"Sunny?"

Her name was a raspy caress. "Drew?" She heard the chair creak again, then felt his weight sink onto the side of the bed. His hands reached out in the dark, as if they had eyes of their own, circling around the sides of her naked breasts, around her back, and up to cup her head in his large hands. His mouth found hers, and with a sweet tenderness, pulling a whimper from the back of her throat, he kissed her. Drew was here, in her house, in her arms, his mouth mating with hers—not with hot passion but with tenderness, with a communication of deep understanding, with a gentle healing of the terrors and torments of the day.

Lowering every barrier, Drew spoke. "Sunny, I love you. More than words can tell, more than life." His mouth slanted over hers again, slurring the words.

Sunny wondered if she was dreaming. She arched against him, wanting to feel the texture of his skin against her breasts.

She pulled her mouth from his. "Drew?" Her hands reached up, caressing his face, tracing the outline of his lips. He nibbled her fingers.

Sunny glanced down at herself. "I'm not dressed for company."

"Good. I'm not company. I like you the way you are." He paused significantly. "Change that to: I love you the way you are. I'd like to keep you this way for the next year. Maybe by then I could get my fill of you, but I don't think Joe would appreciate it."

"Where is Dad? Does he know you're up here?"

"Yeah. I can't say I really have his blessing, but he didn't try to stop me. Besides, he has his hands full trying to keep the reporters at bay."

"Reporters?"

"You're the talk of the town once again. Instead of rescuing a child, this time you were a hostage."

When she started to speak, Drew broke in. "I need to tell you something." Drew reached over and turned on the bedside lamp, illuminating the room with a soft glow. His hand drifted to the plane of her hip. He gazed into her eyes, conveying his love without words, reading Sunny's response as if they'd been communicating as a couple for years.

He cleared his throat. "You were right, Sunny. I'm

only handicapped in my mind. But as of today, that's over. It's something we need to talk about sometime, but if you're willing, I'd like to wait until another time. There are a lot of other, more important, things I want to tell you.''

When she nodded, he tipped his forehead against hers. ''I love you with all my heart. I have for weeks, but I couldn't let myself follow through. I had too many things to settle in my own life and heart first. I'm sorry for the pain I've caused you, for the way my words have wounded you. I wish I could take every one of them back and offer you nothing but happiness, but that's not what life is always about. I had to learn, we both had to learn about each other the hard way. This love that I have to offer you has not come easily to me.''

Sunny reached up, trying to still his words with a caress across his lips.

He took her hand, tucking it against his neck and turning his head to capture it. ''Let me say this, Sunny.''

Sunny whispered her lips across his before she looked up at him, waiting.

''I do love you with a love I never believed could exist. I want to spend the rest of my life with you. I want to see my child swell your belly and suckle at your breast. I want to grow old and gray with you and enjoy our grandchildren. I want to make love with you every night until death comes between us. There is nothing else on earth, except death, that could separate you from me.''

A shiny tear traced down her cheek. Drew captured the tear with his mouth, taking it for his. He crushed her against his body.

Sunny pulled back a little and looked into his eyes. ''I love you, Drew. Together we can build a lifetime of dreams.''

SHARE THE FUN . . .
SHARE YOUR NEW-FOUND TREASURE!!

You don't want to let your new books out of your sight? That's okay. Your friends can get their own. Order below.

No. 92 TO LOVE AGAIN by Dana Lynn Hites
Cord thought just one kiss would be enough. But Honey proved him wrong!

No. 93 NO LIMIT TO LOVE by Kate Freiman
Lisa was called the "little boss" and Bruiser didn't like it one bit!

No. 94 SPECIAL EFFECTS by Jo Leigh
Catlin wouldn't fall for any tricks from Luke, the master of illusion.

No. 95 PURE INSTINCT by Ellen Fletcher
She tried but Amie couldn't forget Buck's strong arms and teasing lips.

No. 96 THERE IS A SEASON by Phyllis Houseman
The heat of the volcano rivaled the passion between Joshua and Beth.

No. 97 THE STILLMAN CURSE by Peggy Morse
Leandra thought revenge would be sweet. Todd had sweeter things in mind.

No. 98 BABY MAKES FIVE by Lacey Dancer
Cait could say 'no' to his business offer but not to Robert, the man.

Meteor Publishing Corporation
Dept. 193, P. O. Box 41820, Philadelphia, PA 19101-9828

Please send the books I've indicated below. Check or money order (U.S. Dollars only)—no cash, stamps or C.O.D.s (PA residents, add 6% sales tax). I am enclosing $2.95 plus 75¢ handling fee for *each* book ordered.

Total Amount Enclosed: $_____.

____ No. 122	____ No. 81	____ No. 87	____ No. 93
____ No. 76	____ No. 82	____ No. 88	____ No. 94
____ No. 77	____ No. 83	____ No. 89	____ No. 95
____ No. 78	____ No. 84	____ No. 90	____ No. 96
____ No. 79	____ No. 85	____ No. 91	____ No. 97
____ No. 80	____ No. 86	____ No. 92	____ No. 98

Please Print:
Name _____

Address _____ Apt. No. _____

City/State _____ Zip _____

Allow four to six weeks for delivery. Quantities limited.